Tremble

The Enchanted Journey Book One

ROSA LEE JUDE

ISBN-10:1942994001
ISBN-13:978-1-942994-00-8

Rosa Lee Jude
Visit my website at www.RosaLeeJude.com

Books by Rosa Lee Jude

The Enchanted Journey Series
TREMBLE
JASMINE
NEVERWRONG

The Legends of Graham Mansion Series
(with Mary Lin Brewer)
REDEMPTION
AMBITION
DECEPTION
SALVATION
REVELATION

Chapter One

THE DREAM WAS always the same. She was in a lush garden. Encircling her was a forest. Yet, all the colors were wrong. At her feet, the grass was purple. Above her, the sky was yellow. Flowers floated by without stems. As she reached out to touch one, it squished in her hand, like the paint of an oil painting. Birds would fly by, swooping low near her head. They would hover in front of her, as if waiting for her to speak.

Further in front of her, in the mist just beyond her view, she would see someone with an outstretched hand silently beckoning her. It seemed to take a long time for her to walk the short distance. Just when she thought she was close enough to see who the person was—

"It's 7:15 and sunny at WPRT and here's Morning Mandy with the latest weather."

"7:15! What the…?"

Tremble Dawson sat straight up in bed and reached for her alarm clock. The numbers were flashing, a sure sign that the electricity had flickered off during the night and messed up her alarm clock. Power surges seemed to follow Tremble wherever she lived. It was one of the many weird occurrences that surrounded her life. Because of this phenomenon, Tremble normally set a battery-powered backup alarm. The late working hours of the past few days had gotten her off schedule. Now, she would pay for her neglect.

"I can do this. I can get ready in five minutes."

Tremble began talking out loud to herself as she jumped out of bed and reached for her cell phone. Talking out loud calmed her. She needed calm. She needed a gallon jug of calm these days. Tremble began punching numbers on her phone as she fell over an ottoman covered in magazines. It had been a rough week and it was only Wednesday.

"Jillian? Yeah, this is Tremble. I've overslept. You have got to stall the meeting."

Jillian Andrews was the receptionist at the advertising agency where Tremble was interning between her junior and senior years of college.

Tremble frantically ran into the bathroom and turned on the shower as she listened to Jillian ramble on with chastisements about being late.

"Miss Dawson, do you know how many *serious* career-minded young adults applied for the internship that you are going to be late to?"

"No."

Tremble jumped out of her pajamas. For a split second, she considered taking the phone into the shower to save time.

"One hundred and thirteen *punctual* young adults."

"I know. It's inexcusable. But, you've got to help me."

"I do not *have* to do anything but my job. I am not the one who is in trouble. But, I will help because I realize how important this meeting is to everyone."

Tremble looked in the mirror and assessed the damage. One eye looked like she'd been in a fight. All of the previous day's mascara and eyeliner made a ring around it. The other eye was naked. The hair wasn't too bad.

"Thank you. I am so grateful. I will be there as soon as I can."

"Tremble, remember who this morning's presentation is for. This is one of the most successful cosmetic companies in the world. Appearance counts."

"I thought it was via video conferencing." A wave of new panic came over her.

"It is. That makes it even more important for you to look your best. It's like you will be on television."

"Okay, Jillian. I've got to go."

Tremble didn't wait for another question. She dropped the phone on her clothes hamper and jumped into the steaming water. It might be the fastest shower she would ever take. She needed to buy time to carefully apply her makeup.

Tremble was given the opportunity to assist the president of the advertising agency during the making of a multi-million dollar proposal to land the contract with one of the top cosmetic companies in the world. Tremble was so nervous about it that she had bought an entire new collection of makeup so she would have the face of Infinity Cosmetics.

After stepping back out into the room of steam, she made a small hole in the mirror. Her hand was shaking with nervous worry, but she managed to fairly flawlessly apply the high-end products. Quickly, she moved on to her hair—jet black with natural streaks that almost gave it a purplish tint. It was one of her best features. It was a direct contrast to her mother's sandy blonde hair or her father's mousy brown. Neither of them seemed to be able to tell her from who her ebony locks had come.

Normally, she would have curled her long hair and allowed it to cascade down her back. But a quick brushing was all there would be time for. She pulled her hair back into a loose ponytail and finished getting dressed, staggering into her small kitchen as she put on her best black heels.

"Choo Choo, I am so thankful that I worked late at the office and left the work there. I can't imagine what I would do if I was late and my boss didn't have the presentation to use."

Tremble talked to her apricot toy poodle as she grabbed a slice of bagel. Choo Choo wagged her tail in agreement. As Tremble pushed the button on her Keurig with one hand to make a cup of Kona coffee, her other hand pulled a container of low fat peppermint mocha creamer out of the fridge.

After quickly walking Choo Choo, filling her water bowl, and giving her a small treat, Tremble gave her precious friend a loving scratch behind the ears and closed the door. A quick glance at her cell phone told her it was 7:40. Not bad. Maybe she would only be fashionably late. Her heels clacked on the steps as she rushed down the three flights of stairs, carefully holding her coffee mug away from her. Her mind raced. Who was she kidding? There was nothing fashionable about her lateness. She couldn't afford it, but she decided to take a taxi. It was her only hope.

A little luck fell upon her. Someone was getting out of a taxi just a few feet from her building. The handsome older gentleman heard her cries and held the taxi for her. He nodded to her as she got in.

"286 James Street."

Tremble had a strange feeling of déjà vu as the man closed her door. He gave her a gentle smile, and she realized that he was the spitting imagine of the late comedian Robin Williams, albeit an older version. She almost told the cabbie to stop the car as it sped off. As she turned and looked through the back window, there was no one on the street.

KALEIDOSCOPE ADVERTISING built its business on catalog creation. In its earliest years, the agency published all the major department store catalogs, including Sears and JC Penney. With the onset of the Internet era, producing printed wish-books became a thing of the past, but that didn't stop the firm from thriving. Quickly adapting to technology, Kaleidoscope became a leader in getting those same companies and dozens of others to put their inventory on the World Wide Web. Keeping the web sites current and attention grabbing was more work than making printed books. The agency's business grew as fast as the medium it was using. It thrived on new, fresh ideas and looked to the next generation to help create the latest cutting edge campaigns. Internships with Kaleidoscope were competitive. If a student made the grade, he or she was almost guaranteed a position with any serious advertising agency in the country. Tremble was amazed that she had made it through the screening process. When she landed the sole summer position, she felt that the sky had opened and graced her with golden light.

Racing into the five-story building that housed Kaleidoscope's floor of offices, Tremble nodded at Henry, the doorman. During her first few days of work, she thought the gentleman's daily sentry position at the entrance was outdated and old fashioned. Now, several weeks later, she realized that it was just another of the intriguing things about the building and its occupants that seemed surreal. Once through the doorway of 286 James Street, it was like stepping into another time.

Her cell phone told her it was 8:15 as she got onto the elevator. Many professional office buildings had updated historic structures with modern elevators. But, 'The James,' as the building was called, had kept the elevator and many other reminders of its original design. Each morning, Tremble read an engraved plate on the elevator wall that proudly displayed 'Otis Elevator Company' and the year 1955. She was thankful that the fifties were the era when push button control systems had replaced the manual handling of elevators. She learned that tidbit from Henry. She estimated that he was in his late seventies. He had worked there his entire adult life.

The elevator doors opened at Tremble's top floor destination. A straight line from exiting the elevator led her right to Jillian's circular desk. Jillian, retro personified, was in her late forties. Her appearance gave the impression that she lived long before her time. Tremble often expected her to suddenly change into black and white as if the woman had walked into an episode of *I Love Lucy*. For the most part, Jillian was all business. She arrived at the office each morning at seven and fielded dozens of calls before most of the associates had even drunk their first cup of coffee. Tremble heard that the agency partners had tried to promote Jillian, but she insisted on staying right where she was. "I am the heart of Kaleidoscope," she told Tremble on her first day. "Everything must come through me."

"They are in the main conference room. It seems that the gods are on your side today, Miss Tremble. The company representative who will be viewing the presentation had a family emergency and will not be calling in until eight thirty."

"Then I suppose I have two minutes to tell you that blue wiggle dress is divine."

Tremble leaned over the counter to get the full view as Jillian stood up and smiled. Her wardrobe was breathtaking. Tremble passed by several vintage shops near her college campus, but never ventured into one before meeting Jillian. Knowing that being on the woman's good side would be a huge plus, she began spending time on the weekends investigating the shops and researching 1950s era clothing. Her ability to describe Jillian's outfits with the correct terminology seemed to impress the woman, being tardy obviously did not.

"I felt it was appropriate for the importance of today."

"I thought you said the presentation was via video conference."

"Yes, my dear. It's not the only important thing that shall happen today. You better get your little tardy self on down the hall. I told CeCe and Bridget that you were detained this morning because of a bout of nervous stomach."

Jillian gave Tremble a big smile. Her red lipstick was as perfectly applied as the heavy black eyeliner that graced her eyes.

Tremble hurried down the hallway toward the conference room. She stopped outside the glass wall and looked into the room. On either end of a long conference table sat the two owners of Kaleidoscope, CeCe Rider and Bridget Bartholomew. Between them on each side were several very tired looking associates. Everyone had been working overtime to prepare for this potential client.

The story was that the two women were college roommates who magically turned their individual talents into a successful business partnership. CeCe was tall, slender, and had long straight black hair reminiscent of Cher in the 1970s. She was all business and was in charge of the sales and financial side of the company. Rumor had it that there were a long list of ex-husbands in her past; trading up was her motto, and a slick sense of humor sometimes left you wondering if she was kidding or not.

In stark contrast, Bridget was short, round, and blond. She had a Bette Midler kind of persona, with a quick wit and funny demeanor. Every conversation with her included a joke and most of her sentences ended in sarcasm. Bridget had been married once. Her husband died in a car accident one year to the day after returning from two tours during the Vietnam War. She had told Tremble about him during the first week of her internship. It had been an unusually serious conversation that had arisen from Tremble telling Bridget how Jake, Tremble's long-term boyfriend, had left suddenly to enlist in the Navy. The conversation seemed to make Bridget melancholy.

"All I wanted was for Terry to come home alive from Vietnam. It was all I ever prayed for, all I thought about. Then, he did and I stopped wanting anything else. I forgot to keep on wanting him to stay alive. I gave up my hoping because I thought I didn't need to anymore."

The words had lingered on Tremble's thoughts. Sometimes, she wondered if that was why Bridget never married again. But the energy she wasn't putting into love, she did put into creativity. Bridget's designs were legendary and were what had put Kaleidoscope on the map. She could take the dullest of subjects and make it jump off the page. With the ability to add movement and sound that the Internet offered, Bridget's web site designs would almost reach through the screen and make the viewer press the purchase button. They seemed magical.

A SIGH OF relief passed over Tremble as Maureen Kensington, the Vice President of Advertising for Infinity Cosmetics, accepted the proposal.

"It's brilliant; simply brilliant, ladies. I've always heard that a campaign by Kaleidoscope is like money in the bank. Make room on your mantel, Bridget, I'm sure you will be taking home another Clio for this one."

Bridget laughed and nodded. "Oh, Maureen, thank you. But, those dust collectors are already taking up too much space in my bookcase."

"Yes, I've heard that Meryl Streep says the same thing about the Oscars that clutter her home. The advertising world is full of envy. It isn't every agency that has multiples of the world's most recognizable advertising awards. Infinity will be the envy of our peers for landing Kaleidoscope."

"Thanks, Maureen, but Infinity doesn't have peers. You have companies who dream of being your peers. I'll be in touch next week regarding the details of the contract." CeCe took over the conversation. "We appreciate the opportunity to work with Infinity. Hope your daughter's arm heals quickly."

With a click of a button, CeCe ended the conversation. The two owners stood up and air high fived each other from their respective end of the conference table and each did a little dance. Tremble was caught off-guard by the sudden change of mood.

"It's a tradition. They always do that when they land a new client." Keith, a junior associate in the agency, leaned over and whispered to Tremble. He looked like a Ken doll and from what Tremble had been told, by some of the women in the office, he had a long line of Barbies in his past.

"Let's all break for an early lunch." CeCe stopped dancing and addressed the group. "We will caucus about our next steps and assignments back in here at three o'clock sharp." CeCe cut her eyes toward Tremble. The stern look was followed by a wink.

"Clear your heads. Breathe in some fresh air. We need our creativity to be flowing this afternoon." Bridget's comments were always positive and Zen-like.

Tremble was surprised the presentation had taken so long. Three hours had passed. She was getting hungry and needed to shake the feeling of anxiety that had overtaken her morning.

"Jillian, I am going to Carmichael's to get some lunch. Can I bring you anything?"

"Now, Tremble, you know that I pack my lunch every day— cottage cheese and pineapple. I've got to keep working on this figure if I am going to fit into these dresses."

Jillian ran her hand down her side. Tremble could have sworn she heard the theme music to *Leave it to Beaver* playing in the background.

THE LATE JULY sun was warm on Tremble as she sat at the window of Carmichael's. The small bistro was a favorite of the young professionals who worked in the downtown business district. The sandwiches were unusual with movie star names and farm-to-table ingredients. The salads were Tremble's favorite and she ate one almost every day.

It was warm, too warm for her to be feeling a chill come over her as she ate her Cobb salad and caught up on her email. She shrugged it off until she started feeling like small slivers of ice were being stuck into her back.

"Hey, Tremble."

She knew that voice, deep like a base drum and smooth like silk. It glided over her. Icy chills moved down her back. She imagined that steam was rising over her head. As she turned to look at the speaker, her eyes followed from the shiny black shoes up the white pants to a white starched uniform coat with lots of buttons, white gloved hands held an equally white hat with a large dark brim. Tremble caught her breath.

"May I sit down?"

All Tremble could do was nod. Her heart was beating faster than her mind could form words.

"I guess you're surprised to see me. It's been quite a while."

"Three years."

Tremble heard her response and thought how surreal the number seemed. Three years since she had seen Jake. It was incredible.

"Yes, it has all been kind of like a dream. A dream in fast forward. It passed so quickly. I moved from one training to another, from one assignment to another. This is the first time I have been home on leave in all that time. My mother has been furious. But, she and Dad have visited me."

He looked down at his hat. For a moment, Tremble forgot that one summer day after they graduated high school, Jake had suddenly enlisted in the United States Navy. She forgot that the only serious boyfriend she ever had, before or since, had broken her heart. Her mind could think that way. Her heart was a different story.

"I tried a couple of times to write to you. But, I swear, Tremble, each time I wrote a letter something happened to it. It was like it disappeared before I could mail it."

Tremble rolled her eyes. Did he think she was an idiot? She returned her gaze to her lunch. The hardboiled egg slice in her salad looked like a happy face. It was a welcomed distraction.

"I didn't know what to say to you. I couldn't seem to figure out how to explain what I had done. I imagined you were still mad. I can't say that I blame you. I don't know why I treated you that way." Tremble remained silent through his rambling. "I was wrong. I had to see you when I came home. I had my Mom call yours to find out where you were."

Tremble looked back up. She noticed his crew cut and smiled inside. His hair had been so important to him, now it was gone, just like she was from his life.

"Are you going to talk to me at all or just give me the silent treatment?"

"You look good, Jake. The Navy agrees with you."

"You're still mad. I knew you would be."

Tremble had to get out of there. If she stayed much longer, her true emotions would come out. She'd lost her appetite anyway. She stood and picked up her tray.

"No, I'm not mad. I've accepted your decision."

She began to walk toward the line of trashcans against the wall. Jake followed.

"That's what I came to talk to you about. I wanted to tell you that I was wrong. I shouldn't have disappeared like that. I don't know what came over me. I should have told you that I enlisted. I should have explained my reasons."

Before turning to face him, Tremble allowed a small smile to cross her face.

"No, Jake, I think you were right. You've got dreams to pursue, and so do I. Our dreams don't seem to be travelling the same path."

She touched his jacket. Tiny red sparks came from her fingertips. It made her feel lightheaded.

"I graduated in the top of my class in every training from boot camp on. I'm going overseas for a little while." He paused. Tremble saw a sternness briefly pass over his face. "When I return, I get to choose where I am stationed next. It's like a reward." Jake touched her. "I was thinking that maybe I could pick a base near wherever you might be thinking about living. In case, maybe, well, you might consider—"

There was a time, not so long ago, when these words would have filled Tremble's heart with joy. But, somehow now that she was faced with them in reality, a sadness filled her.

"I've got to get back to work, Jake. Thanks for coming to see me."

Jake followed her and continued talking.

"So that's it. You won't accept my apology? You won't give me another chance?"

Without turning to look at Jake, Tremble answered him.

"You can't just summon a chance when you want one, Jake. I think you've had your share already."

TREMBLE COULD FEEL the sparks coming from her fingertips as she walked away from Carmichael's. The sparks seemed to be especially prevalent when she was emotional. It was a troublesome habit that no doctor seemed to be able to explain as she was growing up. It hadn't really bothered her until she realized that the other children in her classes didn't experience the same. Her parents assured her that it wasn't that noticeable. Since no one had ever mentioned it to her, she presumed they had been right.

Returning to the office, Tremble found Jillian still at her desk. Afternoon was normally a busy time for the receptionist, as calls from all over the United States would light up the phone lines. Tremble paused for a moment as she spied CeCe pacing in her all-glass office. She seemed to be having quite a heated debate with a man dressed in a white suit.

"Who's that in CeCe's office?" Tremble asked Jillian.

"No one is in CeCe's office that I am aware of." Jillian stood and looked in that direction. "CeCe is on the phone, she has her headset on."

"But, there's a man sitting there in front of her desk; he has on a white suit, a very white suit."

"Tremble, are you feeling okay? The only person I see in that office is CeCe." Jillian sat back down at her desk and answered a call. "Kaleidoscope Advertising, this is Jillian, how may I help you? Oh, how are you, Mr. McGuire? I'm sorry; Bridget is presently out of the office. May I take a message or could someone else be of assistance?"

Tremble walked toward her own cubicle as Jillian continued talking to the customer. Every few steps she would glance toward CeCe's office. Each time she would see the man in the white suit. Even though his back was to her, she could tell that he was young and handsome.

"It's been a strange day. Maybe I need more caffeine."

Tremble mumbled to herself as she left her desk and headed to the break room. She found a fresh pot of coffee. As she returned to her cubicle, she was startled to find CeCe sitting in her chair.

"So, you are seeing men in white jackets today?" CeCe got straight to the point.

"No, I just saw one man in your office in a white jacket."

"But, while you were out to lunch, you saw another man in a white jacket, did you not?"

Tremble looked at her in amazement.

"Well, yes, how did you know that?"

"Tremble, what I am about to say is not going to make any sense. It will actually sound like nonsense. But, please listen and do what I say. It will all make sense soon enough." Tremble held her breath as CeCe paused. "It's time that you asked your mother for the letter." Tremble started to speak, but CeCe held up her hand to stop her. "Go home and ask your mother for *the* letter. Don't ask me a lot of questions; I cannot answer them right now. Take the afternoon off. Contact your mother, and ask her for the letter."

"But, we have our brainstorming meeting is afternoon. Don't you want me to be a part of that?"

A feeling of fear overcame her. Perhaps, being late was more serious of an offense with CeCe than Tremble had realized.

"Don't worry about the meeting. It is only the beginning of this project. The conversation with your mother is far more important than Infinity Cosmetics."

Tremble's vision began to blur and her head started to pound. CeCe was not making any sense.

"This has been a very strange day. I don't understand what you mean. You don't even know my mother, do you?"

"Yes, Tremble, I do. You will understand later. For now, go home and ask your mother for the letter. Trust me." CeCe paused and look intently at Tremble. "Don't worry, your job is fine."

As CeCe walked away, Tremble sat down at her desk. Her mind raced. What in the world could her mother have to do with all that was happening? What sort of letter could she possibly have that CeCe would know about?

"I must be going crazy." Tremble mumbled.

"You're not crazy." Tremble jumped as CeCe spoke to her from the other side of the cubicle wall. "Today will be a day of discovery for you. Life will never be the same. It's time for you to know. Go home."

"And ask for the letter."

"Yes, exactly."

"WHO IN THE world names their daughter Tremble anyway?"

Tremble talked to herself as she paced the floor of her mother's house, the house Tremble grew up in. The walls of the hallway were covered with photos of her immediate family—her mother, her father, herself. It had always puzzled her why she never saw photos of anyone else—no aunts or uncles, no grandparents, no cousins, no friends from days gone by. It was as if her mother, father, and she were the only people in their own little world.

After CeCe sent her home, Tremble stopped at her apartment to pick up Choo Choo. The dog loved car rides and loved the backyard of her family's house even more. Tremble walked through the kitchen and looked out the window. Choo Choo was frolicking around the backyard in hot pursuit of a squirrel. The sweet pet was the last present she received from her father before he died. Choo Choo was priceless to her.

"Tremble, what a wonderful surprise." After almost an hour of waiting, Tremble's mother, Dana, walked through the door.

Tall and slender with blonde hair in a pixie cut, Dana Dawson looked more like a model than the office manager of a large medical complex. It was the same office where Tremble's father,

Andrew, began his medical practice when Tremble was just a baby. He had taken permanent medical leave when Tremble was seventeen and lost his battle to cancer just a month after her high school graduation. The past few years had been hard.

"It's been a crazy day, Mom."

Tremble was the first to start the hug. Mother and daughter, tall and short, they were polar opposites in so many ways. The glue of the family had been her father. Now, they had to hold on to each other just a little tighter.

"It must have been for you to make a trip out here on a Wednesday."

It was a forty-five minute drive to the suburbs from the city where Tremble lived and went to college. Visits home were usually relegated to weekends or holidays. But, it wasn't often that your boss told you to go see your mother. Especially when you didn't know that they knew each other.

"You want to tell me about it?" Dana kicked off her shoes, washed her hands, and began to make a pot of coffee. It was one habit the two shared. "Oh, I see Choo Choo is with you." Dana pressed the brew button and walked to the back door. "Come on in here, little girl."

Choo Choo made a beeline for Dana and was quickly in her arms giving her kisses.

"She misses you."

"I miss her."

"You should get yourself a dog."

"I've thought about it." Dana put Choo Choo down and returned to the kitchen, rewashing her hands. "Let's see what I can find for us to have for dinner."

As her mother began exploring the contents of the refrigerator, Tremble sat down at the kitchen counter. The kitchen was very open with a high ceiling. The walls were painted a soft celery green, which complimented the white cabinets with glass doors. Stainless steel appliances completed the look. An extra large kitchen island served not only as a food preparation area and sink, but also as a meeting place in the vast room.

Dana became engrossed in planning the impromptu meal. This was the way she operated. Tremble's mother rarely pressed about whatever was bothering her. Instead, Dana went on with normal tasks and left the conversation open. It was a successful piece of psychology.

"I was late to work this morning. We had this big presentation to do for Infinity Cosmetics. I stayed at the office until almost ten last night working on it."

"Hmmm, did you oversleep this morning?" Dana pulled out a package of chicken and began to unwrap it.

"Not exactly. I was tired, no doubt, and I slept like the dead. But, my alarm clock must have briefly lost power during the night and got unset. I was so tired last night that I forgot to check my battery-powered alarm. Thankfully, I had my battery radio programmed to come on at a quarter after seven. I like to hear the weather in the morning while I am getting ready."

"Just like your father." Dana turned toward her daughter and smiled.

"So, I was late to work, but it turned out okay as the person we were presenting to was late as well." Tremble watched as her mother began to speak. "I know that's still no excuse for being late. Really, it is not a habit of mine."

Tremble paused for a moment and watched as her mother began mixing up a marinade for the chicken.

"So, anyway, the presentation was very successful, and Kaleidoscope landed the account."

"That's wonderful. And, your work was a part of that?"

"Yes, Bridget had me create the entire visual presentation. It was all done via videoconferencing. Bridget, of course, was doing the presenting. The graphics were all my work."

"Excellent. That should be a feather in your cap."

"Yes, this internship has been wonderful. I'm still amazed that I even got an interview for it."

Tremble watched Dana's face carefully as she made her last statement. She was beginning to think that there was a hidden connection between her mother and CeCe.

"The chicken will need to stay in the marinade for about thirty minutes or so. Can we continue this conversation in my bedroom as I change clothes?"

Tremble poured each of them a cup of coffee and followed her mother.

"Jake came to see me."

Dana stopped in the middle of the hallway that led to the bedrooms, turning slowly to face Tremble. "Oh, that was a surprise, yes?" A concerned look engulfed Dana's face.

"Oh, yes, it was a surprise to me. But, I understand that you were aware of the possibility." Tremble paused as Dana raised her eyebrows. "He was all starched and handsome in his Navy uniform."

"Well, I suppose Jake would look good in a uniform. For the record, his mother called me about two weeks ago and asked what you were doing these days. She did not mention that she was on a discovery mission for her son."

Dana took the mug of coffee that Tremble offered her and continued walking toward her bedroom.

"He wants a second chance. He says he is sorry for what happened."

"And what do you want?"

Tremble paused and pondered her answer. "I'm not really sure, Mom. I thought I knew Jake. I thought we had a future. But, when he just up and enlisted with no warning, it was like he was a totally different person. He really seemed sorry today, almost like he didn't know why he had done it. My trust in him has been severely damaged. I just don't know." Tremble hadn't realized how she felt until the words came out of her mouth.

"Don't be in any hurry to decide. See how things progress on their own. My strong daughter will do the right thing. So, today was quite exciting. Let's have a quiet dinner then and watch a movie."

"That sounds good. Then you can tell me about the letter."

In a flash, the very air changed. Tremble felt a coldness overcome her. Her mother stopped moving. Dana was completely still, too still. They had almost reached the bedroom. The slate blue walls seemed to be closing in on them. It was as if they were suspended in that moment, frozen. Tremble watched as her mother slowly turned around to face her. Dana grabbed hold of the doorframe.

"Mom, you are scaring me. Are you okay?"

As Dana's face came into full view, Tremble got her answer. Dana's eyes were filled with tears—tears and fear.

"What did you just say?" Dana's voice was almost a whisper.

"I, I said you can tell me about the letter. Mom, I didn't mean to upset you. CeCe said I should ask you about a letter. It was all very strange today at the office. I came in and there was a man in CeCe's office, only no one else seemed to be able to see him."

"How was Jake dressed today?"

"I told you. He was in his dress uniform. He was all starched and formal looking. Mom, are you okay?" Tremble reached out to her mother as Dana slowly slid down the wall to the floor. Tremble grabbed the coffee mug out of Dana's hand. "Mom, say something, you're scaring me."

Setting the coffee mugs down on a hallway table, Tremble kneeled and was pulled into Dana's waiting arms. Her mother squeezed her so tight.

"I have dreaded this day your entire life. After your father passed, I couldn't imagine how I would face this alone. I've been thinking that maybe since he was gone, perhaps they decided I could keep you."

"Mom, you are not making any sense. Maybe we should take you to the doctor."

"No, Tremble, it's time that we had a very long talk."

Chapter
Two

ANA LOVED CLOCKS. They were all through the house. One of the largest wall versions was in the dining room. As Tremble sat across from her mother at the table there, the tick-tick-tick sound on the wall behind her was almost deafening. She imagined that her nerves were wound as tight as the springs within it.

In her mother's hand was an envelope. Tremble could not remember seeing an envelope that color before, it was black, and yet, it wasn't. It seemed to change colors. Or was that her eyes playing tricks on her?

"Tremble, before I give you this letter, I want to explain something to you."

The last time her mother spoke in such a serious tone was when she told her that her father was dying. Tremble shuddered to think what could be coming next.

"When Andrew first got out of medical school, he worked

on the trauma team at a hospital about an hour from here. We had only been married about a year and were trying to start a life and pay down our student loans. We both worked as many extra hours as we could. We lived in this wonderful old house. It belonged to a delightful elderly lady who had been a widow for many years. Her children lived far away, so she rented part of the house out as two apartments. There was one back entrance with a circular staircase that led up to a landing on the second floor. Then, on each side of that floor was an apartment."

"Mom, this is an interesting story and all, but what does it have to do with this letter?" Patience was not something Tremble had in abundance.

"Humor me, dear; this is all part of it."

Dana set the envelope down, but kept it near her. Tremble could see her mother's fingerprints on the envelope. The prints were glowing. It looked like the envelope was breathing.

"There was a young woman who lived in the other apartment. Her name was Jasmine."

As Dana said the woman's name, a myriad of noises began invading Tremble's head. It was like an orchestra was playing while a computer generated a variety of other sounds. It made her wonder if she was having a stroke or, at the very least, a nervous breakdown. She tried hard to focus past the sound and back on her mother. Dana's lips were moving. Tremble silently told the sound to stop and just as quickly as it came, it left.

"She had actually been the one who told Andrew that the apartment we rented was available. She was a nurse at the same hospital where your father worked." Dana paused and stared at Tremble. She seemed to stare right through her. "She was the most beautiful woman I have ever seen."

In a flash, a vision of a beautiful woman flashed before

Tremble's eyes as if a movie screen was suddenly in her view. As her mother described her, the woman's features became clear.

"She was so beautiful that she almost did not appear real. Her hair was jet black, shimmering like onyx, and it sparkled. Her eyes were the deepest most beautiful blue and there were little starbursts in her pupils. Her skin was ivory, like you might imagine Snow White's would be."

Tremble sat mesmerized by her mother's description as the woman came into view. Now, she knew she must be losing her mind. She rubbed her eyes. When she opened them again, the vision had disappeared. Even though she had never heard the story before, something about it seemed familiar. Glancing down, she saw that sparks were again coming out of the ends of her fingertips. It had been something that occurred off and on all her life. This time, the light they gave off gleamed purple. She balled her fingers into a fist.

"She sounds like someone from another world."

"Tremble, she was." Dana reached across the table and took her hand. "And she was your mother."

It was as if a cold bucket of water had been thrown on Tremble. She recoiled her hand from her mother's and backed her chair away from the table.

"She was my what?"

"Tremble, please try to understand. We never meant to hide this information from you. You have been our whole life since the day you were born." Dana paused. Tremble could see that there was fear and sadness in her eyes. "She was your birth mother. Let me explain it."

"Explain that all these years I have been adopted and no one ever told me?"

Tremble stood up and walked away from the table. Everything started moving. She stopped and stood still, but the spinning continued. She reached for the wall.

"Darling, please sit down and let me finish. There is more to this story than just that."

"Just that I was born to someone other than you and Dad, and no one has told me my entire life? Well, that explains why I never looked like either one of you. I don't think I want to hear any more." Tremble whirled around. The spinning got worse. She didn't think she had ever felt so angry and so afraid. She looked down at her hands and they were shaking. She heard crackling as the power of the sparks from her fingertips increased. "What is happening to me?"

"You need to calm down, Tremble."

Dana walked to her daughter and pulled her down into the chair. As her mother reached for a chair of her own, Tremble lunged for the letter.

"What is this going to tell me?" Tremble tried to open the envelope and dropped it suddenly. "What is wrong with me? That feels like it is 100 degrees. Is it what is happening to my fingers?"

Dana picked up the envelope. Tremble noticed that her mother appeared to not have any trouble holding it.

"Calm down. This will subside if you just try to calm down."

"You know why this happens, don't you? You've always known. All those doctors that Dad consulted with—"

"Let me finish telling you. Then you will understand. Well, you will at least begin to understand." Dana took a deep breath and looked deep into Tremble's eyes. "Okay?"

Tremble nodded. What choice did she have? She placed both of her hands in her lap and tried to stop shaking. The sparks subsided. The spinning stopped. The fear continued.

"We became friends with this woman, our neighbor. She began spending a lot of time with us, especially me. She confided that she was pregnant, and then she told us her story."

JASMINE SAT ON the long green couch across from Dana and Andrew. Her raven hair spilled over her shoulders and almost touched her growing belly. Her deep blue eyes were the color of star sapphires with flickering starbursts especially visible when she laughed.

"Please, listen carefully to what I am about to tell you. I would like for you to adopt my baby." Jasmine paused and waited for a reaction. She saw a stunned look cross Andrew's face and a slight smile cross Dana's. "I ask for nothing in return except the promise that you will raise her and protect her as your own. I have chosen you very carefully and think that you are the ideal ones to raise my daughter."

"Daughter?" Dana said. "You know that it is a girl?"

"Yes, I am positive."

"Why do you want to give her up?" Andrew's voice sounded nervous. "I mean, I don't mean to offend you; you just don't seem like someone who would give her child away."

"I will be glad to explain my reasons, but you must agree to adopt her before I can tell you the entire story."

Dana and Andrew looked at each other. "I think that Dana and I will need to discuss this before we can give you a decision."

"Very well, I will give you twenty-four hours."

"Just one day? That isn't long enough to make such an important decision."

Andrew stood up. At first, he started to head for the door, but he hesitated and stood in the middle of the room.

"I believe that you will be able to decide. You either will want this child or you will not. Please come back to my apartment tomorrow night."

Jasmine led the couple to the door. As they were about to pass over the doorway, she again began to speak.

"I understand your hesitation. You do not understand my reasoning. But, please allow me to be clear and direct. The two of you were carefully chosen by me. I can imagine no one else being able to raise my daughter in the manner that befits her destiny. These words may appear strong to you now, but they shall be fully understood by you when you agree to become her parents. I know that you will not make this decision lightly."

It was all that Dana and Andrew talked about from that moment on. They stayed up half the night weighing the pros and cons and trying to figure out why their beautiful and enchanting neighbor would want to give up her daughter. Where was the father? Where was Jasmine's family? Where would Jasmine be while they were raising this child? It all seemed very strange, and yet, it all seemed so right.

"You've reached a decision?"

Jasmine turned and moved slowly away from the door as Dana and Andrew entered her apartment the following evening.

"Yes, we have," Andrew sat down beside his wife on the couch. "We have some questions."

"I must know your decision first, before I can answer any questions."

"But there is one very important one that we feel we need an answer to, only one."

Jasmine looked deeply into Dana's eyes and nodded her head.

"If we raise this child, where will you be?"

"Far away, you will have no interference from me."

Jasmine ran her hand over her belly. Dana could see a tear run down her face.

"Will this child ever meet you?"

Jasmine paused and thought for a moment.

"I would like to think that I will see her again, once she is grown, but there are many things that shall influence that. It may not be meant to be."

TREMBLE SAT IN shock as her mother told the story. It was so hard to imagine that she had once belonged to someone else and that this person had given her away. Her feelings of anger toward her parents now began to turn and align themselves with this beautiful stranger.

"I don't think I care anymore." Tremble rose from her chair and walked toward the living room window. "Why should I care about her; she didn't want me? I don't care what that letter says; you are my mother."

"Darling, that is wonderful to hear. And, yes, I am your mother in the truest sense. But, you must not pass judgment until you hear the rest of this story."

Tremble sat down on the couch with her mother and began to listen again as Dana continued.

"So, DO I understand clearly that you shall be this child's parents?"

Jasmine paced back and forth in front of Dana and Andrew. She wore a long skirt that swished as she walked. It was made from crinkled taffeta in a gorgeous fuchsia color. Her blouse was of a similar fabric and color with lace and beads in black and silver complimenting the design. Her presence was captivating.

Andrew and Dana looked at each other, and he took his wife's hand as he answered. "Yes, we will."

"Very well, I thank you. This news relieves a heavy worry on my very soul." Jasmine stopped her pacing and sat down in a rocking chair that was opposite the couch. She pulled a long black shawl around her shoulders. She seemed relieved, a load lightened from her. "It is time for you to know why."

Jasmine closed her eyes and put her hands on her stomach, a whirl of fog began to grow around her and Dana let out a small cry. Jasmine opened her eyes and tilted her head to the side smiling.

"I came here from another world—a parallel universe to this time and place. Some of the humans from this time and previous times live with us and travel back and forth."

Andrew's grip on Dana's hand increased and Dana could hear him swallowing deeply.

"I am an enchantress, a witch as humans would say."

Jasmine's words caused Dana to gasp. She immediately covered her mouth, trying to conceal her reaction.

"I am sure that you find this shocking, but in my world everyone is either an enchantress or an enchanter, a witch or a warlock. I come from a magical world." Jasmine looked intently at Dana and Andrew, then nodded her head and continued. "Humans find it hard to imagine that there are other worlds beside their own. I do not mean what I am about to say as insulting, but it is a universal truth. Humans are not the most advanced species. Your world has not progressed enough to be able to handle universal understanding. Your species still needs more layers of perception. This is why Earth is a good place for other species to hide when they are in trouble. It is very easy to adapt to life here and because of your belief system, we are not suspected."

"Belief system? I don't understand what you mean." Andrew looked puzzled.

"Humans have become very advanced in many ways, in rudimentary science and technology, in medical advances, but you don't seem to have the capacity to believe in things that are magical. And magic is the fundamental building block for the entire universe. We believe in a Supreme Being, but we know that this being's power is magical and that magic touches everything that was created." Jasmine paused and breathed deeply. "In the world that I come from, my family and my husband's family are very powerful. Many in our land did not want us to marry. But, our love was strong and we were united. Our years together have been few. The heritage of my people is steeped in prophecy. We believe that this child may be the fulfillment of one of those prophecies. Because of this, her very life is in danger. My husband and I decided that we did not want to risk what might happen. Until she is grown, he and I will go into hiding. We believe it is the only way that we can protect her."

"Why would anyone want to harm your child?"

Dana's tone did not conceal her revulsion to the thought. Jasmine looked at them both. She seemed to be searching for the right words to convey her message.

"This may be very hard for you to grasp. It is a key aspect though that you must understand. My husband and I are the most powerful enchantress and enchanter in our world. Our daughter will be even more powerful. We must protect her. We must let her grow up without this knowledge. When she is older, then it can be decided what her destiny will be "

Dana and Andrew sat in silence trying to grasp what Jasmine had just told them. Andrew was the first to break the silence.

"All of this is a little too much to comprehend. Why should we believe it?"

Jasmine stood up and Dana could see that this simple movement was becoming harder for her. The weight of the baby was hindering her mobility.

"You want proof. That is understandable."

Jasmine closed her eyes and began to slowly whisper, it was melodic and soothing with an undertone of power. The sound began to quicken and the air in the room changed, there was warmth and cold at the same time. It was as if the very atmosphere was changing. Jasmine opened her eyes. There, before them, stood a white panther, long and sleek. Dana screamed and Andrew jumped up as if to shield his wife, an action that did not escape the notice of Jasmine.

"Do not be afraid. Our feline friend is but an illusion. I could create the real thing, but that would take more energy than I can afford to use at the present time."

To prove her point, Jasmine walked through the white panther, and Andrew and Dana realized that, while lifelike, it was an illusion they were viewing, like a hologram.

"Satisfied?"

Andrew nodded and Jasmine snapped her fingers and the panther disappeared. As Jasmine laughed, Dana realized that her laugh sounded like wind chimes, lyrical and ominous.

"Pregnancy has altered my powers somewhat. That is one of the reasons that I came to live in the human world. My safety was in question. My powers are mainly being used to protect this child."

"You mentioned earlier that you are from a parallel universe.

What do you mean?" Andrew's questioning was not over.

"I come from a world that is very close and yet very far way. It parallels the world here in many respects; it is an *Earth* with many similar characteristics. We have land, trees and sky, and animals. Some are quite different from those you know. Our beings are divided into males and females as well and our roles are similar, but we are immortal. We are further advanced in the ability to manipulate and use our senses and powers. Our senses exceed the five you know." Jasmine stopped and watched Andrew and Dana. "For example, I know that your brain is processing the words I just said. You are mentally considering them. You are emotionally weighing them. But, for me, I can take that a step further. I can feel them. My mind is literally travelling back to my home and taking in some of the things I have just mentioned. I am picking my favorite flower. I am smelling its beautiful aroma and tasting the color while I express the thought."

"Wow." Dana's voice could not conceal her amazement. "And this child will be able to do that? I'm not sure we will be wise enough to know how to raise such an advanced child."

A look of pure joy crossed Jasmine's face. "This statement pleases me so much. It tells me of the deep love that I imagine you will give this child. When she is born, I will put a spell on her that will suppress some of her powers. Not all of them. That is impossible. But, it will lessen them to prevent accidents. In our world, babies frequently conjure very interesting things during their toddler years. Baby jabber is filled with magic." Jasmine's laugh filled the air. She moved slowly across the room, sat beside Dana, and held her hands.

"I am so glad that I met Andrew at the hospital. None of the other mortal couples I have observed seemed right. This was the third city I had been to, and I was becoming concerned that

I would not find the right couple."

"How will the process work?" Andrew stood and walked to a window. He seemed a little uncomfortable with the female bonding that was occurring before him. "There will need to be a formal adoption."

Jasmine rose and stood across from him. "Indeed. I have already consulted a lawyer and paid all the fees for the process. When the birth occurs, the birth certificate shall be issued with you as the parents. I shall have no mortal claim to this child."

"Mortal claim?" Andrew glanced at his wife.

"No legal claim to the child in your world. If she ever returns to my world, the adoption will not mean anything there."

"So, we would lose her?"

Jasmine turned to Dana and saw the tears in her eyes.

"Somehow, I do not imagine that will ever be the case. You will love and nurture her. You will be her mother, even if she comes to my world at some point. Magic cannot break your bond with her."

Dana smiled as the emotion of the moment left her eyes.

"I am becoming tired. Let us pause our discussion for now. I will make arrangements for you to meet with the lawyer and for the bank account to be set up."

"Bank account? You didn't mention that we would have to pay anything for this child." Andrew looked Jasmine straight in the eyes.

"Oh, my goodness, no. I am setting up a bank account for you, for the child. You will never have to pay for anything she will ever need or want. There will be money for her daily needs, medical needs, everything. In the next few weeks, a house will be bought of your choosing. Her home shall be your home."

"I don't know what to say. We intended to provide for this

child." Andrew seemed embarrassed by his previous reaction. "We didn't expect to be paid."

"I am providing for my child. It will be more of a labor than you can imagine, providing material things is the least I can do."

Jasmine walked to the rocking chair and sat down. Her energy seemed to be waning. Her glow was dimming.

"A labor of love." Dana walked toward Jasmine and knelt in front of her. "Do you know that I cannot have children?"

Jasmine took her hand. "Yes, I know. It is the sadness in your aura. This child shall lift that sadness and make you whole."

Dana was overcome with emotion. Her words came out in a whisper. "I shall love her as my own."

"She shall always be ours, yours and mine. Our bond shall come through her heart."

TREMBLE STARED AT her mother. She couldn't imagine that she didn't biologically come from her. There had been several physical characteristics that did not match at all, but her parents always shrugged it off by saying that she looked like some long dead distant relative. Being someone else's child, however, would certainly explain some of the strange things that had happened in her childhood.

As a child, one of her punishments was that she was forbidden to watch television for a period of time if she had misbehaved. Consequently, her father would turn the TV off and no one would watch. Tremble remembered, at the age of six, she was especially interested in watching *Little House on the Prairie* reruns when she came home from school each afternoon. Her father had a rare day off from the hospital the day she came home with her mid-year report card. It had a "C" in Math and a note that said 'Tremble scored well on all of the tests, but she only completed half of her homework.' This was totally unacceptable to her father and TV timeout began.

That didn't set well with Tremble, so she announced in a calm, but firm, tone that she wanted to watch TV. Her father again said no, actually said it several times. As her mother entered the room, Tremble stood up, and with a dramatic flair, lifted her arms up over her head and in a booming voice said, "I want to watch TV!" Instantly the TV came on to the appropriate channel with Michael Landon smiling on the screen. Her parents were so shocked that they didn't try to turn it off again. They left the room to talk in whispered tones.

Children think they have magical powers. These episodes in her childhood were little hints to her not-so-mortal heritage, but it didn't register with Tremble. Now, she had no choice. She had to accept the story her mother had just told. There was no denying that magic had made itself known throughout her life. Tremble had not recognized it. Now, she must learn more about who she really was.

Chapter Three

"**S**O, WHEN CAN I read the letter?"
Tremble's voice was hesitant as she wasn't sure that she
wanted to know the contents.

"Let's take some time and step back from this. Let's cook
dinner and relax a little."

Tremble followed her mother into the kitchen. As she
watched Dana take the marinating chicken out of the refrigerator, Tremble's mind flashed back to another example of the
magic that had been hiding in plain sight. The instance occurred
in that very kitchen.

As Tremble recalled, she was around nine and had to prepare
a model of the solar system for science class. She and her father
had worked for hours over several weeks carefully making each
planet. Then, they created an exhibit to show how each related to
the other. On the morning that it would be delivered to school,
it was setting on the kitchen table awaiting departure. There was

a small space beside it where Tremble ate her Rice Krispies that morning. As she listened to the cereal's signature sounds, she commented that she wished the planets could orbit like the real ones did. She made a dramatic abracadabra movement with her spoon and instantly the Styrofoam planets began to move. Both her parents stood in awe as the movement continued until Tremble took another bite of her cereal. She vaguely remembered an admonition from her father that it would be best if she didn't do that at school because the other children might get jealous.

"That smells good, Mom."

The chicken was sizzling in the skillet as Dana slid the last of the vegetables she had been chopping in to join it. Experience told Tremble that her mother would add the rice noodles that were soaking on the counter at the last minute to complete the dish.

"It doesn't hurt for a girl to have one of her favorite dishes on a rough day, huh?"

Dana smiled, but Tremble saw the lines of worry creasing the edges of her eyes.

"Comfort food. I should have known this day was going to be crazy the way it started."

The memory of the man who had offered her his cab resurfaced. It gave her a chill.

As the meal simmered, Dana and Tremble sat on opposite sides of the high counter. The envelope lurked just out of Tremble's peripheral vision. She swore that it twitched every now and then.

"Jasmine was very clear about the circumstances at which time you were to open the letter." Dana seemed to sense where her daughter's mind had returned. "I'm not sure if she could see the future or if she planned to manipulate it. That part of her story was unclear. But, she did say that you might ask for the letter before it was time. That unknown forces might find their way to you and try to influence you."

"These 'unknown forces' you speak of, they sound like they are straight out of Hollywood."

"Well, I suppose, in a way that is a correct comparison. This world that Jasmine came from is beyond my imagination. As good and pure as Jasmine appeared to be, I have no doubt that the forces she wanted to protect you from were equally evil. Whatever threat forced your mother to come to the human world was serious enough that she was willing to leave her child with strangers to protect her." Dana paused and shook her head. "Please understand this, Tremble. Your mother did not give you up easily. It was a horrible time for her. Yet, she believed that harm would come to you if you stayed with her. Your safety was her primary goal. She wanted you to have a chance for a happy childhood and to be safe until a time when she might be able to see you again."

Tremble could tell that the last words were a little painful for her mother. She imagined how she must have felt to raise a child as her own with the understanding that the biological mother might one day return and take her love away.

"You are my mother," Tremble looked Dana in the eyes. "I don't care what happens. No one replaces you, or Dad."

Dana reached across the table and took hold of Tremble's hand. "I know that. I do not worry about Jasmine returning to your life. We can learn to share your love. I worry that the forces that want to harm you still exist."

"So, how are you supposed to know when to give me the letter?"

"First, you are supposed to ask for it."

"Okay, did that. Now what?"

"You are supposed to tell me about something specific that happened to you on that same day."

"What is it?"

"I can't tell you that. You have to tell me."

"Well, I got up late. I was involved in a big presentation at work." Tremble paused to see her mother's reaction. Seeing none, she continued. "Jake came to see me and that was certainly a shock. I thought I was past any feelings for him, but then he looked all-handsome in his Navy uniform. I can't imagine how he can possibly keep that white jacket clean. He always spilt stuff every time he ate."

Tremble stopped when she realized her mother had visibly winced at the mention of the white jacket.

"That's it, isn't it? The white jacket! Jake was wearing a white jacket. Then, the man in CeCe's office was wearing a white jacket, too."

Dana took a deep breath and shook her head.

"I have carried this information inside me for a very long time. I was the secret keeper in this family. I dared not reveal those kinds of details to your father. He couldn't have kept it secret if his life depended on it."

Dana paused and smiled. Tremble did the same. Her father always looked like he was going to burst when there was a secret to keep.

"So many nights I prayed that this day would never come. At the same time, I prayed that Jasmine was safe. I couldn't have it both ways."

Dana picked up the envelope that had been lurking beside them. Tremble thought she heard a buzzing noise coming from it. She could see a little light trying to shine through. Dana motioned for Tremble to follow her. Upon entering the living room, she pointed to the couch and Tremble sat down. There was a small storage area behind a door in the coffee table. Tremble knew that it was where her parents had always kept a locked firebox. She thought that might have been where the letter had been kept, but she had not seen her mother retrieve it earlier. Now, her mother was unlocking the lock box and removing a DVD from an envelope that was marked 'Tremble.'

"Before your father died, he recorded a special message for you. He wanted me to play it for you, if the time should ever come that you would learn your true identity. It hurt him so when he knew he would miss special turning points in your life." Tremble choked back tears. "But, your father was especially sorry to miss today. Tremble, your father and I never wanted to keep this information from you. We told Jasmine that we would be fine raising you with the knowledge that you were adopted. Jasmine was resolute in her admonition. She said that your knowledge of who you were would disrupt the protection spell she put on you at birth."

"Protection spell. What? I'm under a spell? Oh, this is making my head hurt."

Choo Choo jumped up into Tremble's lap. Her sweet dog always seemed to know when she needed extra comfort. Tremble's mind raced. The emotions that were going through her were overwhelming. She wondered how long it would take before her system would just shut down from the overload.

"I wouldn't disagree with you. It's a lot to take in at once. After you were born, Jasmine asked to be left alone with you for a few minutes. Everyone left the room." Dana fiddled with the remote control of the DVD player. "I couldn't stand it. I wanted to see what she was doing to my daughter." Dana paused. "In my mind, I was your mother from the moment Jasmine said I could be. I wanted to know what she was doing."

"And? Did she have a cauldron brought in to make some nasty brew for me to drink?"

"Tremble. I will not have you speak that way about your mother. You hear the word 'witch' and immediately think of the wicked one from Oz or the Halloween costume version. Those are only fairy tale characters. I have met a real enchantress, actually several, and they are beautiful, charming, and intelligent. They radiate kindness and power, but are still humble and fragile. Some of them have delightful senses of humor."

"Several? You have other 'witchy' friends besides Jasmine?"

"Once again, I do not like that tone, Tremble. You will not be disrespectful. Jasmine used the terms 'enchantress' and 'enchanter.'"

"Okay, whatever! Can I watch this DVD now?" Tremble paused. She could feel the grumpiness growing within her. Patience was not her strong suit. "Although, I am not sure how I feel about seeing and hearing Dad."

"It will be hard, but it was very important to him to be able to prepare you when the time came. Please understand that I am going to leave you alone while you watch. It was your father's request. He wanted this to be a private conversation between you and him."

"I wish we would have had this conversation while he was still here."

"He would have preferred to, but it was not possible. He actually hoped that you would never see this. He hoped that your past would leave you in the present." Dana rose and handed the remote control to Tremble. "I love you, my dear. I will be upstairs in my bedroom when you are finished and are ready to open the letter."

As Dana left the room, Tremble stared at the huge flat screen television in the living room. Her father loved technology. Each of their bedrooms and the family room all had large screens. She smiled to herself thinking how many times she had come home to find her father chatting away with a delivery crew. Her father had been a surgeon and specialized in putting people back together again after horrific accidents. He could reconstruct the intricacies of the human body, but never quite mastered programming a VCR.

She took a deep breath and pushed the play button. She gasped as she saw her frail near-death father smiling into the camera. "Is it on, Dana? Okay, good. Now you leave me. I need to speak to Tremble alone."

Choo Choo barked as she heard a voice from the past. "Yes, that's our Daddy." Tremble's eyes welled up with tears as she hugged her dog close.

"Tremble, my dear daughter, if you are watching this, then two things have happened. One is that you have asked for the letter, and the time has come for you to learn about your heritage. The other is that I have passed away and am, regrettably, not there to help you through this important passage."

Tremble wondered how something could feel so bad and so good simultaneously. It hurt her so to see this man she loved so much in such a frail state, knowing what the outcome would be. It felt so good to see him—the man she loved so much on the hardest day of her life.

"No, that's not true," Tremble said out loud. "The hardest day was the day I lost you."

"Your mother, I'm sure, has by now told you how we met Jasmine and what she asked of us. I am sure that you are more than a little angry about it all." Andrew smiled and Tremble saw the man who could find humor in anything. "You must know that it was the hardest and easiest decision of our life together. It was also the decision that forever changed us. You never asked why you didn't have any siblings. It might not have mattered to you. But let me tell you at least a part of the story, because it will now help you understand how deeply we loved you and especially how important you are to your mother."

Tremble watched as her father fiddled with the oxygen tank beside him and put the plastic tubing around his face. She remembered this time frame. The cancer had firmly set up residence in his strong body and was making him a shell of his former self. Andrew breathed deeply several times before continuing.

"When your mother was sixteen, she and her parents were in a horrible automobile accident. You've seen her family albums and know that her parents died in that accident. What you do not know is that your mother was injured very seriously. She had to be put back together again. She and I had started dating about a month before the accident. My mother took me to the hospital and sat with me as we waited for Dana to come out of surgery. My mother had grown up next door to Dana's father and they were childhood friends. We prayed and prayed that the doctor would work a miracle and save Dana. And that is what happened, and that was the day I vowed to become a doctor just like him."

Smiling at her father's resolve in that statement, she realized that her parents' love had started young and survived tragedy. It began to be clear to Tremble that she knew very little about her parents' life together aside from her own life with them.

"But your mother's internal injuries were severe; the doctor's talent kept her alive, but not without the loss of several internal organs, including one kidney, part of her colon, and her uterus and ovaries. She would not be able to have children. We had every intention of adopting and sharing our love with a child. We even talked about a special needs child. We had no idea that our child would have magical needs." Andrew chuckled and began to cough.

"I did extensive research on Jasmine. Background checks and even hired a private investigator; much to the disappointment of your mother, she trusted Jasmine from the start. There was no record of her existence before she began working at the hospital. It was as if she had not existed in our world. She was an excellent nurse, and on the night you were born, she told me that she was a healer in her world. It was amazing what she could do with patients. She could calm them almost to a sedation level with just the touch of her palm on their forehead. It was her calm confidence in your mother and I that freed us from the worry that we were not worthy of raising such a special child. Our love for you began before we ever heard your name."

Tremble wondered if her father would talk about her name and how she got it, but realized that his message was almost over as he began to speak again.

"I hope that this letter will provide the answers to the questions that you have and those that we had as well. I hope that whatever evil was lurking from which you needed strong protection has now been destroyed. I hope you will have a wonderful life wherever this new knowledge takes you. You were a gift from the gods to your mother and me. We never for a moment thought anything less. I was blessed to be in your life. I am saddened that my time is over." Andrew bowed his head and took in another deep, deep breath. "But, I must ask one thing of you, one promise. Whatever happens to you now, wherever you must go, please remember your mother. She is not the woman who birthed you, but she is the one who gave you a life. You will always be in her heart. You will always be in mine."

The DVD clicked off and Tremble sat there, once again staring at the screen. She wanted to scream at him to return but knew that it was useless. He was gone, again.

Tremble wasn't sure how long she sat there in deep thought. Dana found her daughter sitting in the same position she had left her. So much time had passed that the DVD player had turned itself off.

"Are you okay?" Dana's voice was a whisper.

"I don't think I want to see the letter now. I don't need to see it. Actually, I don't have any desire to know what it contains. You are my parents. This is my life. Case closed. I don't want to live in a magical world." Tremble stood up and walked toward her mother. "I'm hungry. Let's eat."

Dana seemed stunned at Tremble's reaction. She followed Tremble as she walked into the kitchen. "Tremble, I'm not sure that this is entirely up to you. Jasmine indicated that—"

"Are you saying that you want me to leave?"

Tremble twirled around. She could feel the sparks coming off of her again. Looking down, she noticed that gold was the color they had taken this time.

"No, darling, I don't want that at all, it's just that—" There was a knock on the door. Dana turned toward it. "I'm not expecting anyone, are you?"

"Oh, if it's Jake, I'm not here."

Tremble took a plate down from the cabinet and began slinging food on it. A strip of chicken went flying through the air and landed right in front of Choo Choo. The dog looked up at Tremble, seeming to ask for permission before she gobbled the bite up. Tremble followed her mother to the edge of the doorway where she could, from a concealed view, see and hear who was at the door.

Dana opened the front door. In front of her stood a very handsome young man, in a white jacket, and it was not Jake. "I am here to see Tremble."

"I am her mother. Who are you?"

"I am her Protector."

Chapter Four

TREMBLE WAS LURKING in the kitchen where she could see and hear what was transpiring between the mystery man and her mother. She could see that Choo Choo had taken up a position of guarding as well when Dana came to find her.

"That young man in there is—"

"Gorgeous." Tremble finished her mother's sentence.

"Yes, you are quite correct on that front. The young man is beautiful. I'm not sure exactly why he is here. I'm pretty sure where he is from though. Jasmine told us when it was time for you to read the letter, others would arrive to help us. She also said that dangerous forces might also make their presence known. You need to be on guard."

Tremble nodded. She didn't want to meet this person. She could only assume with the way the day was going that he had something to do with the world of magic. It was all too much, too soon. Reluctantly, she followed her mother into the living room.

Both Tremble and Dana were surprised to find Choo Choo sitting on the man's lap. It almost appeared as if they were having a conversation. Dana cleared her throat. Choo Choo jumped down as the young man rose and bowed.

"May I ask your name?" Dana stood in front of Tremble.

"My apologies, I presumed that you had been informed. My name is Laken."

As the man talked to Dana, Tremble took in his appearance. His features were so perfect. He looked like an airbrushed photo of a model only he was three-dimensional.

"And, you are here to see Tremble, for what reason?"

"I am her Protector."

"That's what I thought you said earlier. I don't understand."

"Ah, well." The self-assured young man they had initially seen suddenly seemed uncomfortable. "I thought that you would have been informed in some manner. CeCe indicated that you would have been prepared by now."

"You are the person who was in her office today, aren't you? I couldn't see your face, but you are definitely wearing a white jacket."

Tremble moved around her mother and closer to the stranger.

"Yes, this is white jacket day. There were very strict instructions regarding my apparel."

Laken smiled at Tremble. In an instant, it seemed as if the whole room lit up. It was not an entirely pleasant feeling that she had.

"Why are you here?" Tremble's tone was direct and unfriendly.

"I am your Protector."

"You've said that already." Dana rejoined the conversation. "What does that mean?"

"I was born on the same day as Tremble. My birth was planned to coincide with hers so that this day would come, and I would be her Protector. I have been aligned with her our entire lives. My existence has been modeled for this role. I am here to protect her."

"Protect her from what?"

"The forces that pledged to destroy her even before her birth." Laken paused and waited for a reaction. "Didn't Tremble read the letter?"

"No, not yet; we've had some other things to discuss first." Dana sat down in a chair and motioned for Laken to do the same. When he did, a strange look crossed her face.

"What is it, Mom?" Tremble sat down in the chair beside her mother.

"I, well, I just had a déjà vu moment, I suppose. I was just remembering Jasmine."

"If you will excuse me for being forward, I think it is time that Tremble read the letter."

"What is the rush?"

"She needs to read the message."

"The message? What do you mean by that?" Dana began to wring her hands.

"Ma'am, I know that this is very troubling to you, and I understand. But I cannot reveal what is in the message. I only know the aspects that concern my work. I do know that we have reached the hour of revealing, and we must not tamper with the timing. It could detrimentally affect the spell that has protected Tremble all of these years."

"Okay, I don't want to interfere with anything that Jasmine put in place."

"Mom, really? You are going to just accept this that easily."

"Tremble, Jasmine gave your father and me a sacred trust. She put all her confidence in us to take care of you, to raise you, and protect you. We have done as she has said all these years. Now is not the time to stop trusting her. This young man must be doing her bidding. I don't think we have any choice at this point."

"I have to do this, don't I?" Tremble took a deep breath.

"I'm sorry to say, but I think you do." Dana put her arm around her daughter. "In my heart, I know it will be okay. Jasmine knew what she was doing when she brought you here to us. She knew what she was doing when she put the spell on you when you were born. And, she has planned what is happening now. It is time to read the letter and find out why this very handsome young man is sitting in our living room." Dana smiled and hugged Tremble. "He is fortunate that your father isn't here; he wouldn't allow him within ten feet of you."

Tremble nodded and took another deep breath as she stood up. Laken matched her movement. She watched as he bowed and extended his hand.

"Allow me to begin again. My name is Laken. I am your Protector."

Tremble looked at him intently. His looks were astonishing, there was no doubt. Yet, there was something else about him that intrigued Tremble more. She could not put her finger on it. It was a feeling, a mixture of feelings—excitement, wonder, fear. She reached out and took his hand, sparks began to fly. They both looked down and saw them. There were distinct blue sparks emitting from their two joined hands. It was magical. A nervous laugh exchanged between them as they released their grasp.

"Hello, I'm Tremble."

"Words I have imagined you saying a thousand times. I have looked forward and dreaded this moment for my entire life."

Laken motioned for Tremble to sit down on the couch. She obliged. Choo Choo jumped up and sat between them, tail wagging for attention.

"Dread? Why would you dread our introduction?"

"Because my job will now begin, what I have been groomed for, the reason for my whole existence. The dread is not in the task; it is in the potential for failure. Your life is now in my hands." Laken bowed his head.

"What if I don't want my life to be in your hands?"

"It is beyond your control. This is our destiny."

"Laken, is there anything that you would like to talk to us about before Tremble reads the letter?"

Dana caught her daughter's eye and gave her a reassuring smile. Laken thought for a moment.

"The letter, I imagine, shall give the best rendition of the story. I may be able to fill in some gaps and answer questions."

"You don't know what the letter says? I find it hard to believe that someone who, as you say, was 'groomed' to be my Protector does not know its contents."

"No, I was born the same day as you were. It is my understanding that this letter was written by Jasmine shortly before your birth, and the only copy that exists is the one given to your parents. I do not think that anyone saw the letter but Jasmine. It is protected by a spell."

"A spell? Why would the letter need protection?"

"Primarily from the curiosity of your parents, I would assume." Laken looked at Dana. She smiled. "It's only natural that they would want to know the contents of a letter that would tell their daughter about her heritage."

Tremble looked at her mother. "Did you ever try to open the letter?"

"I did not." Dana glanced at Laken. "But, of course, your father did."

"Really?"

·"Now, Tremble, you know how your father was. He was a surgeon. He wanted to know what was going on inside something. It was only natural that he wanted to look inside that envelope. He also could not stand secrets."

"What happened when he tried? Did it re-seal itself?"

"The letter caught on fire, big flames. Your father was forced to drop it immediately," Dana laughed. "Remember the scar on his left hand."

"Yes, he said he got it doing surgery."

"Yeah, well, he considered that surgery."

Tremble shook her head, remembering. "Did it catch anything else on fire?"

"No, as soon as he released it, the flames disappeared. He learned his lesson; he didn't try again. Jasmine was clear when she gave us the letter. It could only be opened by you and at the appropriate time."

"I know it is hard for you to understand, Tremble," Laken interrupted. "But spells are very precise. When they are cast by someone as powerful as Jasmine, they are pure and tamper-proof."

"So, Jasmine is the Queen of the Witches?"

"Your mother is indeed a Queen. Even though she has been in exile for many years, she is the Queen of the Kingdom of Neverwrong. It is her birthright to wear the crown. Your father is King, by his marriage to her."

"Okay, Laken, you don't need to be so dramatic. You are making it sound like she is from some other world, some fantasy place. I am not quite convinced that this 'Kingdom of Neverwrong' is not some remote European land that I just never learned about in geography class."

Tremble shook her head as she got up and walked toward the large picture window.

"You do not believe me."

Laken's voice became strong and dominant. The meek and mild side of him had disappeared again. It was replaced by a formidable young man. He looked displeased with Tremble's comment.

"The Kingdom of Neverwrong is very real. I will have to show you."

Chapter Five

THE NORMAL VIEW from the front window of Tremble's house was of a large brick Colonial home across the street where the Garland family used to live. Their oldest daughter, Tabitha, had been Tremble's babysitter. But, as Laken pulled back the drapes, Tremble did not see the edge of a Japanese maple on the left hand side of the window or the evening sun setting on the right. Instead, she saw the most beautiful place she had ever seen. The sound of her mother gasping seemed far away as Tremble took in the view.

The colors were so vibrant. They glistened like fresh paint on a canvas. Only nothing seemed to be the color that Tremble expected. The grass was purple and the sky was yellow. The bark of a tree was red and the leaves were black with silver. The flowers did not have stems. Instead, they seemed to be floating on air and were constantly moving. One such flower kept floating closer and closer. Its center was a deep green and its petals were chocolate brown. She wanted to taste it. She wanted to touch it.

"Go ahead. Reach out, Neverwrong is not just to be viewed, it must be felt."

Laken walked up behind her. Tremble momentarily let her gaze leave the window as she felt Laken's hand gently touch the small of her back. She wondered what color sparks were emitting from his hand, as she could feel them on her back. He nodded as he met her eyes.

"Go ahead."

Tremble reached out her hand.

"Tremble, I don't know if you should." Her mother's voice instinctively made her stop.

"Don't worry. I would never allow anything to harm her." Laken removed his hand from Tremble's back and extended it to Dana. "You can touch it, too."

"How will I possibly be able to have the same experience as Tremble?" Dana walked up behind her daughter.

"You will not. You will have one that is uniquely your own. Tremble's experience will be natural. You shall experience the magic of Neverwrong a different way."

"How will that be?"

"You are able to see Neverwrong now because I have cast a spell allowing it. The same shall be true of this portion of the experience."

As Laken finished answering Dana, Tremble took hold of her mother's hand, pulling it up toward the window. As Tremble's right hand and Dana's left touched the glass, something extraordinary began happening to Tremble, she started to be absorbed into what she had been seeing. She looked down and the purple grass was under her feet. Multicolored flowers were falling all around her. Bubbles floated by with little insects inside.

A hundred fragrances came at her at once; it was overpowering. It seemed to Tremble as if she could smell every living thing around her separately and all together at the same time. Her eyes were becoming one with the color. She felt as though her body was absorbing the experience. She was feeling it from the outside in and from the inside out at the same time. The spell was broken when she realized she was no longer holding her mother's hand.

"Mom!"

Instantly Tremble was again standing in her living room. She looked behind her to find her mother sitting on the couch with her head in her hands. Dana was rocking back and forth. She looked distraught. Laken was standing near her. He looked very concerned.

"Oh, my darling girl." Dana rose at the sound of her daughter's voice and jumped up to engulf her in an embrace. "Where did you go? You were gone for an hour."

Tremble looked back at the window. The real view had returned. The sun was now setting. Darkness had engulfed the neighborhood.

"I couldn't have possibly been gone that long. It only seemed like an instant to me."

Tremble looked over her mother's shoulder. She had only known Laken for a short time, but she could tell that the expression she saw on his face was fear, pure fear.

"How could you let this happen? You are supposed to protect her!"

Dana released Tremble and turned to Laken. Her voice was louder than Tremble had ever heard it. It gave words to the fear Tremble saw on Laken's face. Beneath his tanned skin, she saw rapidly changing colors. It was yellow, then green, then blue.

"Are you okay?"

Tremble walked toward him. For some reason, she felt drawn to him, a connection. This linkage between the two of them made her almost feel him. She could feel the colors that he was turning.

"I'm not sure. I've never felt like this before." Laken extended both of his hands in front of himself and looked at them. The colors were changing faster and with less distinction. "I have read about enchanters changing color in times of extreme anguish. I've never seen it happen before. It's part of our internal sensory system. Our emotions can come out in shade changes to our skin."

If it hadn't been such a serious situation, Tremble would have burst out laughing. Laken's whole body was changing colors. It looked like disco lights were flashing under his skin. Oddly, the colors were so bright they could even be seen through his clothes.

"Oh, dear, this isn't good."

The color changes grew faster. Tremble ran over and took hold of his hands.

"STOP!"

Every light went out in the house, like someone had flipped the main breaker. Everything was dark including Laken. The color changes had ceased. Tremble could hear her mother fumbling in a drawer for a flashlight.

"Are you okay?" Tremble whispered as she squeezed Laken's hands.

"I am now."

Tremble didn't realize how close he was to her until she felt his breath in her ear as he whispered his reply. Her body tingled all over. Laken dropped Tremble's hands and stepped away as the light from the flashlight shone on them.

"I'll go and check the breaker box. Here's an extra flashlight."

Dana handed the flashlight to Tremble. She gave her a look that Tremble could only translate as a warning. Tremble and Laken stood in an awkward silence as Dana went to the laundry room where the breaker box was located. It was only a minute or two, but to Tremble it seemed like an eternity. Every few seconds, she could see sparks flying from her fingertips. The little lights were almost changing colors as fast as Laken had. The house lit up all at once, and Tremble breathed a sigh of relief.

"Are you okay?"

Tremble looked at Laken. He was moving toward the door as Dana re-entered the room.

"Where are you going? You've got to explain to us what happened. Why was Tremble gone so long? What happened to you?"

Dana moved like a football player running interference as she tried to beat Laken to the door.

"I think I need to check in with my supervisor."

Tremble could see that Laken was avoiding making eye contact with her mother.

"Your supervisor? I don't understand."

"Well, that's not exactly what I would call her, but I thought it would be a term that you would understand."

"Your supervisor is a woman. What would you call her?"

"Her Royal Highness."

"What?"

Tremble moved to the other side of Laken. She and her mother had him trapped.

"I report directly to Her Royal Highness Princess Belladonna. She is your mother's sister."

"My mother's sister? I thought my mother was off hiding somewhere?"

"She is. I do not know anyone who has known her exact whereabouts since before your birth."

"So why isn't this Belladonna person in hiding with her?"

"Your aunt, her Highness, is not in danger."

"Why?"

"Because she did not give birth to the heir to the Kingdom of Neverwrong."

"WHAT? I think I better sit down." Tremble collapsed onto the sofa.

"Darling, you are trembling!"

Dana put both her arms around her daughter and rocked her back and forth.

"The prophecy is being fulfilled." Laken began again to walk toward the door "I need to confer with her Highness."

"What prophecy? Stop saying the prophecy is being fulfilled. You are scaring my daughter." Dana's tone was no longer pleasant or even fearful.

"The prophecy says that the letter shall be revealed and the heir shall tremble and all shall know her power."

"But the letter hasn't been revealed, I haven't read it." Tremble removed herself from her mother's embrace and stood up. "That settles it. I am not going to read the letter. You go tell Aunt Highness that I'm going back to my life."

Tremble began to walk toward the staircase.

"Tremble, listen to me." Laken walked toward her. "The prophecy says that the letter will be *revealed*, not read. The order of things has begun. You have to accept this."

"No, I don't *have* to do anything. You can leave this house now."

Tremble crossed her arms and stared straight at Laken.

"Tremble, I am your Protector. I cannot abandon you. You

cannot order me to do anything. I am bound by a spell created by Queen Jasmine. I cannot force you to do anything. You have free will. But, if you go against the prophecy, you will die and everyone you love will die also."

"How can that possibly be?" Tremble relaxed her arms and looked at her mother. Dana just shook her head. "This is all a dream, a very horrendous dream. I am going to wake up tomorrow and everything will be back to normal."

Dana walked toward her. "Your father and I knew that whenever the time came, the revelation would be beyond our imagination. We knew that the truth would be revealed to all of us. Jasmine did not hide that there would be danger. I fear that Jasmine's power has been stretched to the limit by protecting you this long."

"Your mother is right. Our people have not seen Queen Jasmine for over twenty years. She has been in seclusion. Only Her Highness Belladonna knows where she may be."

"What about my father?" Tremble looked briefly at Dana. "Jasmine's husband."

"King Forrest received his royal designation by his marriage to Queen Jasmine. He also descended from the royal line of our kingdom. In human terms, it is a different branch of your family tree. King Forrest's power is mighty and strong, but he also has not been seen since around the time of your birth. It is thought that he might be imprisoned somewhere and that the force who has him is the same one who wishes to see your death."

Laken's words were like a heavy anchor. They slowly pulled Tremble to the floor.

"Before you go to contact Tremble's aunt, I think it is time that she read the letter. I would rather that you be here when she does." Tremble started to speak, but Dana held up her hand.

"Your father and I agreed long ago that it wasn't only our responsibility to protect you, it was also our duty to Jasmine to guide you when the time came. Your mother's care and love has protected you for many years; we cannot start doubting her now. She left you this letter. It is time that you read it."

Tremble allowed her mother to lead her back to the couch. Laken solemnly followed and sat in a nearby chair. Dana sat beside her daughter and handed her the letter. Like her name, Tremble's hand shook as she began to open the envelope. She halfway expected for glitter and moonbeams to burst from it as it was opened, or for trumpets to sound announcing its arrival. Instead, she just heard the crisp sound of parchment and saw a beautiful handwriting in purple ink stare back at her. Tremble began to read aloud.

> My Darling Daughter,
> My heart bursts with joy that you are reading these words, as it means that my utmost dream has been fulfilled. You have remained safe and have grown into a wonderful young woman. My heart knew that Dana and Andrew were the ones who should be entrusted with your care. Their auras were pure and radiated with such love for each other that I knew this combined love would be your best protection.
> But, sadly, this also means that you will soon be outgrowing my spell. This is information that I did not reveal to your parents, as I knew the burden of it would be too great for them to bear. My spell's power could only last until your twenty-first birthday; I imagine that day is very near. Because of this, a Protector has been created for you. His name will be Laken. His purpose will be to guide you as the next part of your life journey begins.
> Make no mistake! Laken is not your servant. He has been taught to protect you, at all costs, even from yourself. Like your father, you may have a streak of defiance that may make you reckless in your behavior. Laken will stand between you and harm and will push you out of harm's way, if necessary. He answers only to your aunt, my sister, Belladonna.

Now, to the portion of this letter that I do not wish to write. Your father and I were selfish. Our love was so strong; we thought that it could conquer all things. We not only naively married, but we allowed our love to create a child who would be cloaked in danger. We both descended from the original families of Neverwrong. Our ancestors were the pillars of the beginnings of all worlds. Legend tells us that there were six sisters and one brother. I descended from the oldest sister, Perpetua. The sisters chose to live their lives in honorable ruling, in pursuing good works, in being fair and humble leaders. Your father descended from the brother, Baldric. His line has been tainted with the hunger for power. Laken and the others shall explain this to you more fully.

Despite these differences, the descendants of the original seven were a united family. As children, your father and I were inseparable. We played from sunrise to sunset and imagined faraway worlds, not unlike the one you have grown up in. During our teenage years, our friendship spilled forth into love. Our parents were against our union. They knew a prophecy foretold that a child would come who would be the ultimate heir of Neverwrong, a descendant of two of the family's strongest lines. They knew that the fulfillment of the prophecy would only bring danger.

Laken will acquaint you with the history of our kingdom so that you can better understand what I am about to say. It is of utmost importance that you learn our history. It is the only way that you will be able to survive the next part of your journey.

Tremble, the hardest thing that I have ever done was to put you into Dana's arms on the evening of your birth. But, yet, as I write these words, I know that there is still yet another meaning to them. It was, at the same time, the easiest thing I have ever done. I knew that Dana and Andrew would give their lives for you, if needed. I know that to be the truth as surely as I know that you would one day be a strong, intelligent, and resilient young woman. I know that you have led a happy childhood. Your protection now must fall into the hands of others and yourself. I will stress again the importance of Laken in your life, as your Protector. He will explain to you what this all means. He will also soon introduce you to my sister, your aunt, Belladonna.

I know that there are probably many more things you are wondering right now and that you have many questions. You will receive your answers in time. Trust Laken and the others who Belladonna has put into place to be your teachers and guides. Learn from them.

Remember all that your mortal parents have taught you. They have made you strong. And, remember, I love you more than life itself. I hope that one day we will meet again. I hope that I can hold you in my arms as close as I have always held you in my heart.

Your mother,
Jasmine

Tremble looked up and saw her mother dab her eyes as she gave her a small smile. Dana's face was full of worry. It mirrored the way Tremble felt. A few feet away stood this beautiful young man in whose hands Tremble had now been instructed to place her life. He looked more like a supermodel than a superhero. An icy fear began to overcome her. The pages fell to the floor and Tremble followed closely thereafter. The weight of the day finally became too much for her body to bear.

"I can't do this. It's too much."

Tremble refused to let herself break down in tears. Her emotions were frozen. She needed to remain strong.

"I need to speak with Her Highness." Laken looked awkwardly at Dana. She motioned for him to leave. "I will return as soon as I can."

After the front door closed, Dana walked toward the stereo system that was connected to their home theater. It was another example of how much her husband loved technology. There were speakers installed in every room of the house that could all be controlled with one remote. His music library was endless, but there was one part of his collection that was very special. She turned it on. A deep and powerful voice began to sing about a tropical place.

"Blue Hawaii." Tremble started to laugh as she looked up at her mother. Dana was doing a hula dance. "Oh, Mom."

"Your father always said that there was no problem—"

"That couldn't be solved with a little Elvis."

Tremble finished her mother's sentence. She got up and walked toward her mother. Dana reached out and took her daughter's hands and tried to get her to dance as well.

"This is exactly what Dad would do if he was here, only I think he would have picked a different song."

"You do?" Dana picked up the iPod and scrolled through the selections. "Heartbreak Hotel?"

"No. Suspicious Minds." Tremble picked up the pages of the letter and sat down on the couch. "Come on, Mom, how can I be the daughter of the Queen of another world? I think it would be easier for me to believe that I was Elvis' daughter."

"Tremble, you just had a glimpse of that world. You stepped into it. How can you deny that? What was that like for you? As scared as I was while you were gone, I was also excited about what you might be seeing and experiencing."

Dana pulled Tremble into her arms. Things were happening so quickly that Tremble hadn't even had time to react to what she had just physically experienced.

"It was all so surreal. It didn't seem to me like any time passed. I thought you were right behind me. It was as if that view we saw absorbed me. I could see and feel everything around me. I could taste the air, it had a flavor." Tremble moved her tongue around her mouth as she tried to remember the taste. "It was like the most delicious, sweet, decadent dessert you've ever tasted and the most savory thing you've ever eaten rolled into one. I could feel the colors pulsing through my veins." Tremble gazed into her mother's eyes; they were large with amazement. "I don't know how else to describe it. The feeling was out of this world. I know that's a cliché statement to make, considering the circumstances. There's really no other way to describe it."

"I can't imagine how many different directions your mind is going right now. Before you were born, I had so many sleepless nights wondering what would happen. Jasmine showed us examples of her power. It was mindboggling and humbling at the same time. Your father told me so many stories of how she would use her powers to help patients. She was truly a healer. She was resolute in her plans for you. The entire adoption process had layers of things to ensure you had a comfortable childhood. Her heart broke the day she handed you to us. I saw her emotionally melt before my very eyes. I knew, as a mother, we would surely see her again. That she would make secret visits to you. But, we have never seen her since."

"What about when she moved? It must have taken her time to do that. Weren't you all still living in the same house that contained your two apartments?"

"No, we bought this house before you were born and moved directly here when we brought you home. But, your father went back to the apartment to see if he could help Jasmine. There was no evidence she had ever been there. Everything was gone."

"What did the landlady say?"

Dana looked intently at her daughter. Tremble could almost see the memories flowing through her. Dana's eyes were darting back in forth as if they were reliving the time.

"She had no recollection that Jasmine had ever lived there. She kept referring to the person who lived there previous to Jasmine. It was the same at the hospital. None of your father's coworkers seemed to remember Jasmine at all. Everything about her time with us vanished. Everything, but you." Dana smiled and pulled Tremble close. "We had to accept that. We knew it was part of her protection. Tremble, we wanted you more than life itself. We knew that even though your arrival seemed like a fantasy, it was the realest thing we had ever experienced."

Tremble paused and thought about her mother's words. She remembered what she learned from her father's video about the horrific accident her mother had been in.

"Didn't anyone ask where I came from?"

"Tremble, there are few people in our lives who knew us before you. Those who did, we told them we adopted you. They didn't ask any questions about your birth mother. Shortly after you were born, your father went to work for another hospital. Our new neighbors, our new friends, they never questioned who you were. You were our daughter. It was as simple as that."

"I still don't understand why you didn't tell me."

Tremble sighed and walked over to the window. The dark street outside looked familiar. There was no evidence of the world she had seen earlier.

"It was an ongoing disagreement between us. Your father wanted to tell you. He thought you should be on guard and ready. I was more in tune with Jasmine's wishes. I wanted you to have a childhood."

Dana paused. Tremble could sense that she was debating whether to say what she was thinking.

"Go ahead. Tell me what you're thinking. Surely it can't be any worse than what I have already heard." Tremble rolled her eyes. "Perhaps, I shouldn't be so hasty with those types of comments."

"For a while, I was afraid you might want another mother. How could I compete with a gorgeous enchantress who had a whole kingdom at her beck and call?" Dana chuckled and shook her head. "I stopped worrying about that a long time ago. I realized that I was the one to be envied because I had you all of those wonderful growing up years. Jasmine was robbed of that.

She had to make a sacrifice that was probably worse than death for her. I hope that the time will soon come that you can have a relationship with her. My worries now are focused on whatever force that she has gone to such great lengths to protect you from all of these years."

Tremble remained silent as she thought about what her mother said. She couldn't imagine going into a foreign world without the security that her parents had always provided her. Yet, she knew that nothing she could imagine in this world would be a match for the force that she had been protected from. Her future was full of unknowns.

Chapter Six

REMBLE ON THE couch and Dana in a chair, each dozed as they waited for Laken to return. Tremble's sleep was fitful, full of dreams that didn't make sense. Choo Choo was a huge yellow cat. Her house was upside down. She could only see Jasmine through a crystal ball. It all made her feel as if she had not rested at all.

As the sun rose the following morning, Tremble opened her eyes. Her first thoughts were filled with panic as her mind began to remember what she learned the day before. Her whole existence was beginning to sound like a fantasy novel. As she stretched and rose from the couch, Choo Choo, lying beside her, jumped up and began wagging her tail.

"Did you go out already?"

Tremble's answer came in the form of her little friend settling down with a half chewed bone. Tremble stumbled groggily into the kitchen and found Dana making coffee.

"Why hasn't he returned? I guess I am going to have to call into work."

Tremble sat down on a stool at the kitchen counter. She had left her phone there the night before to charge. She grabbed it and looked at the screen, but the overwhelming aroma of her mother's orange-almond cinnamon rolls distracted her.

"Oh, how I miss that smell."

"I don't really know when we should expect him. I have no idea how many miles it is to Neverwrong. I mean, how do you get there? I guess we don't know if he actually had to physically travel there or if he could communicate with your aunt some other way."

"You sound rather calm to have not had your coffee yet."

Tremble saw that the coffeemaker was still brewing. Her mouth began to water thinking of the combination of her mother's strong coffee and delicious cinnamon rolls.

"Oh, I've had my coffee. A whole pot of it, to be exact. I am making this pot for you."

"Well, that sounds more like my mother. It also smells like her."

"I thought we needed some comfort food." No sooner had Dana finished her sentence then the doorbell rang. "Maybe Neverwrong isn't as far away as we might think."

Tremble walked toward the front door. But, as she opened it, she was surprised to see that Laken wasn't standing there. Instead, it was her two bosses from the advertising agency, CeCe and Bridget.

"Good morning, Tremble," CeCe said in her smooth as silk voice. "We apologize for the hour, but thought you might need our assistance."

"Ooooh, I was just about to call you."

Dana came up behind her daughter.

"CeCe, Bridget, I thought that you might be joining us at some point. Please, come in."

Hearing her mother's words made Tremble do a double take in her mother's direction

"Good morning, Dana." Bridget's bubbly voice echoed in the foyer's high ceiling. She gave Tremble's arm a little squeeze as she walked by her. Bridget ran her tongue over her lips. "I can taste orange in the air this morning. You must be baking, Dana."

"Yes, you are just in time. I am about to take a large batch of my orange-almond cinnamon rolls out of the oven. Please join us."

"That is very kind of you, Dana. But, we are here to be of assistance to you and Tremble."

CeCe exchanged a glance with Tremble causing her to remember their conversation from the day before. CeCe was the one who told her to go home and ask about the letter.

"You two know about me, don't you?"

"Well, yes. Did you come home and do what I asked you to do?"

CeCe had stopped in the foyer. Bridget and Dana were now watching the exchange between her and Tremble.

"Yes, I did and the young man who was in your office was here last evening."

"I knew that Laken would make his presence known as soon as possible."

"So, you two are from that magical kingdom, too? Is that why I work for you? I thought I got the internship rather easily. I feel like my whole life is a front for this other world. What about my friends and Jake? Are they all just pretend-people in my life?"

Tremble walked in front of all of them and headed straight

to the coffee maker. As she poured herself a large serving in her 'Wicked' mug, she began to wish she had the power to do what the other side of the mug said—'Don't make me call the flying monkeys!' Then she thought, maybe she did.

"Tremble, don't be cross with us."

Bridget's gentle voice floated into the room behind her. Tremble hadn't consciously realized that Bridget's voice had that affect. But, now that she thought about it, her voice did seem to always float.

"Yes, we are from your home world, Neverwrong. We were assigned to watch over you and your parents when you were very young by Her Highness."

"Belladonna."

"Why, yes. Has Laken already filled you in?"

"Yeah, I seem to have an aunt from a magical world."

Tremble had gulped her first cup of coffee and was now refilling her mug. Her mother took the pot out of her hand and offered some to their guests.

"By the way, this is my home world. I don't think I want anything to do with Neverwrong."

Tremble's direct statement caused Bridget to gasp. She watched as the woman sat in the nearest chair.

"Listen, Tremble, I know this is all a lot for you to grasp suddenly, but you might want to cool your heels a little before you make blanket judgments." CeCe had taken a mug of coffee from Dana and set it down to use her hands to make her point. "You are the heir to the throne. You have responsibilities."

"Well, if I am the heir, then I should be able to do whatever I want." CeCe rolled her eyes and began to speak, but Tremble stopped her. "I think I will quit college, form a rock band, and tour the world."

"Tremble, stop talking such nonsense."

Dana's voice now had an edge to it as she pulled the tray of rolls from the oven.

"Why? If I have all this power, I need to learn how to use it, and then I can do whatever I want. All my songs should be hits, right?"

"Actually, Dana, Tremble is correct. She doesn't have to go to college. She could decide that she wanted to be a brain surgeon and she would almost instantly have the knowledge to do that."

Dana gave CeCe a look that could only be described as disgust.

"So, is that why school has always come so easy to me? If I liked a subject, it always seemed like I just knew what the teacher was going to say."

"And, if you didn't like it, you would get a headache." Bridget finished Tremble's thought.

"Yes."

"Tremble, is this true? I always thought that you did some of your homework way too quickly. Then, your report card would come and you would have high marks and I stopped worrying."

"Yes, it is one of the interesting talents of our heritage." Bridget took a cinnamon roll from the plate that Dana held in front of her. "We don't have to learn the way mortals do."

"Mortals? What? Is this an episode of *Bewitched*?"

"Oh, very funny, my dear." Bridget laughed between bites. "Dana, this is heavenly."

"So, still, no one has answered my question. Has my whole life been one big lie?"

"No, Tremble, it hasn't." CeCe walked toward Tremble and took her by the hand. "Please, sit down. Your parents were chosen by Queen Jasmine. She searched for quite some time before she found a couple she believed would love her child as much as she did. She also made sure that this couple would be willing to do anything to protect her child, even allowing strange people to join their lives." CeCe smiled and nodded to Dana.

"Strange people? I don't understand."

"Do you remember Tabitha?" Bridget spoke between bites of cinnamon roll.

"My babysitter? She lived across the street."

"Yes, with her parents."

"Samantha and Darren. Oh, my gosh. I never thought of that before. That's just tacky."

"Well, yes, perhaps. Those two just seemed fascinated with that show, and Belladonna didn't seem to care what they called themselves. She made them pick a different last name." Bridget reached for another roll. "They were some of your guardians during the first years of your life. They were assigned to not only watch out for you, but to also watch over your parents. At first, it was to make sure that your parents did not put you into any jeopardy. Jasmine trusted Dana and Andrew completely. Belladonna is not as trusting as her older sister."

"But, eventually, the Garlands' duties included guarding your whole family." CeCe took over the conversation while Bridget continued to chew.

"Guarding us from what?"

"Tremble, this is a long and complex story."

"Either someone starts telling me something about this force that is out to get me, or this conversation is completely over and you all can fly on back to the magic kingdom."

"Tremble, show a little respect."

Everyone turned to find Laken standing in the doorway. He had forcefulness to his voice that gave his already handsome looks even more charisma. Tremble did not like the way it made her feel.

"You owe your life to Queen Jasmine. You will not disrespect the servants of her kingdom."

The silence in the room became deafening.

"I do not want to disrespect anyone or anything." Tremble stood up and faced Laken. She was not going to back down from him. "I want to know who these people are that I have had to be protected from all my life. I want to understand why in the world that I should leave the only home and family I have ever known because you people tell me that I am the daughter of a queen."

"Laken, it is time Tremble heard the story." CeCe spoke and Bridget nodded. "It's past time for Dana to hear the whole of it, too. Bridget and I have battled over it for years. Dana, we wanted to tell you that very first day that we met you and Andrew. But, Belladonna forbade it."

"Why could we not be trusted with this information when we could be trusted with Tremble?"

Dana sat down on a kitchen barstool. She seemed to have accepted the fact that she needed to be seated when she heard the story.

"Belladonna was afraid that once you and Andrew knew everything that you would give up your assignment." Bridget sat down next to Dana and patted her hand.

"Assignment? This wasn't an assignment to us." Dana slapped the counter in front of her. Everyone jumped. "From the moment we said yes to Jasmine, Tremble was our life. She was the only thing that mattered to us."

"We know that. It was clear to see from the first moment we saw the three of you together." CeCe walked toward Dana. "There was no doubt to us. But, you must remember, Belladonna had not met you. To our knowledge, she has not even seen Tremble."

"And why is that?" Tremble chimed into the conversation.

"Because Her Highness was afraid that she would be followed to this world," Laken answered Tremble's question. "She refused to put you in jeopardy."

"She was also afraid that she would be too tempted to take you herself, if she saw you." Bridget's soft voice sounded like a song. "You are so much like her beloved sister she would not be able to bear the thought of leaving you behind."

"Well, that's nice and all, but it still doesn't explain why someone wants to harm me."

"Go ahead, Laken, that's your cue." Bridget rose from the stool and motioned for them to follow Laken. "May we take the rest of those lovely rolls with us into the living room?"

Everyone picked up their coffee mugs after Dana refilled them. She smiled at Bridget and handed her the large platter that still held some cinnamon rolls.

Once they were all seated in the living room, Laken walked over to the large picture window. As he drew back the drapes, Tremble reached over and took hold of her mother's hand. As before, the view changed from their neighborhood to a beautiful mystical landscape. The colors were lush and fluid and made her want to reach out and touch them.

"Ah, home, it is so beautiful this time of year." Bridget smiled and clapped her hands with delight. "The sap is running on the peppermint trees. Doesn't it smell wonderful?"

"Peppermint trees?" Disbelief could be heard in Dana's voice.

"Take a really deep breath."

Dana did as Bridget instructed. Tremble did also and immediately inhaled the calming smell of peppermint. It smelled like Christmas and toothpaste.

"Oh, my goodness! How in the world am I able to smell that?" A shocked look crossed Dana's face.

"Dana, all beings have the same senses. Humans normally only use five. You possess many more than that and you can extend the uses of some to transcend time and space."

Bridget's voice was so soothing. Tremble wondered if that was one of the reasons why clients always liked her design ideas. Perhaps, she lulled them into acceptance.

"It is true that those from our world are immortal, but our powers come from deep inside our beings. We are similar to humans in many ways. But, our society encourages learning on different levels and the use of multiple senses differently."

"Excuse me." Laken interrupted. "I really think that it is imperative that I begin telling Tremble our story. I also have some important news from Belladonna to convey." Laken paused, as everyone became quiet.

With the blink of an eye, the view through the window changed from the beautiful lush colors to a dark gray-blue landscape. Waves of light quickly passed over it, as if some creature was quickly flying low to the ground.

"When all of the world was first created, it was divided into many kingdoms and lands. Some people think of these kingdoms as galaxies, as portions of a bigger whole universe. There would be parallel realities of magical and non-magical beings or immortal and mortal. Those who were the first to settle Neverwrong were endowed with great wisdom and power. Neverwrong would be parallel with Earth and the humans who abided there." Laken waved his hand in front of the window and the image instantly changed.

"The original rulers of Neverwrong were seven siblings. History tells us that these seven came from within the highest mountain in Neverwrong. They came from the ground, from nature, they appeared out of nowhere, but would rule everywhere. They were wise and fair. They earned the respect and devotion of their subjects. Yet, there was division among them. The oldest was a male, Baldric. His six sisters were Perpetua, Abelia, Crispina, Gwenora, Elsavetta, and Verina."

"My goodness, those names are a mouthful." Dana interrupted Laken. "Tremble, you shouldn't have any complaints about your own name."

Tremble started to speak but decided not to. She nodded for Laken to continue.

"These seven are the pillars of Neverwrong history."

"Where did they come from?" All eyes went to Tremble as she asked the question. "You say that they came out of the mountain from nature. Where had they been previously?"

Laken darted his eyes back and forth between CeCe and Bridget. Tremble could see that CeCe gave him a little shake of her head. It looked to Tremble as if this was a topic they were not ready to discuss.

"The origins of The Seven have been held in secret for centuries. It is something you shall learn eventually, but I do not think it is relevant to our discussion now."

Laken's words were clear and concise. Tremble was seeing a different personality than had come across the night before. This young man would be more challenging to get around than she previously thought.

"In the beginning, The Seven ruled over Neverwrong together. They were each in charge of different aspects of the kingdom. As time passed, they grew a little older and wiser. At some point, an issue arose that caused one of them to begin ruling as the Supreme Ruler, which first was Queen Perpetua. Her name means lasting. Her reign was long and noble. She is your great-great- grandmother, Tremble."

"Tremble, Queen Perpetua is our most loved Royal. She is still held in reverent honor to this day," Bridget smiled and nodded as Laken continued."

"All of the sisters ruled graciously and maintained good relations between their portions of the kingdom. But, their brother, the eldest, was not pure of heart. His strength was battle. Baldric was very mighty and strong. He battled to increase his power and the dominion of his portion of the kingdom. King Baldric did not like the arrangement. He thought that because he was the oldest, and the only male, he should be the Supreme Ruler. He had the reputation for being a difficult man. King Baldric was your great-great-grandfather."

"Lovely. I am a mixture of good and evil. Well, that was an interesting story. What does Aunt Belladonna have to say?"

"Tremble, darling," CeCe answered. "This story has only just begun."

Tremble took a deep breath. Patience was not something that anyone in the human world or the world of her birth seemed to have bestowed on her.

A surge of electricity filled the air and quickly the window came to life. Two large portraits filled their view. One was a beautiful woman with porcelain skin, beautiful raven hair placed artfully on top of her head, and piercing lavender eyes. There were years of life that marked her face, but her beauty was no less diminished. The other was an equally handsome man with a ruddy complexion, chocolate brown hair with flecks of silver, and captivating royal blue eyes.

"May I introduce you to Queen Perpetua, Her Supreme Royal Highness of the Kingdom of Neverwrong?" Tremble gasped as a smile formed on Perpetua's face and she gave Laken a slight nod. "And King Baldric, her brother."

"I do not think that it is a good idea for you to have any interaction with them at this point." CeCe whispered to Dana and Tremble.

"Why?" Tremble's answer was louder than necessary.

"Because, my darling girl, these guardians are of the opinion that I am a bad influence." King Baldric's booming voice grew slightly softer as Tremble looked in his direction.

"She is the daughter of Queen Jasmine and King Forrest. She is several generations removed from your time."

Bridget's voice was no longer floating. It had grown feet and was stomping through the room.

"But, she is so beautiful. She does favor our dear mother. Do you not see the resemblance, Pet? Our youth is coming back to me, as if in a dream."

"Our youth was wasted on your arrogant behavior." Queen Perpetua's voice was strong, but melodic. "This child must deal with the folly of our youth."

Queen Perpetua's voice seemed very familiar to Tremble.

"I have heard your voice before." Tremble stood up and walked toward the window.

"Careful." Laken's hand reached out and grabbed Tremble's arm. She wiggled out of his grasp and walked closer to Perpetua. Gently, she raised her hand up to touch her face.

"Do not do that, my dear."

Tremble quickly jerked her hand away and stepped back.

"Do not misunderstand me. I would like nothing better than to embrace you. But, sadly, I am gone from your time. My existence now is trapped in this portrait. You are not skilled in your powers. If you touch me, you might find yourself within this painting, within my time, without the power to return. Conversation shall be our only form of communication. Perhaps, one day, it will be held within our own kingdom."

Tremble was more confused than ever. This beautiful woman was her great-great- grandmother. It was simultaneously a good and bad feeling. She didn't know how to react.

"Begging your forgiveness, Queen Perpetua, but I believe it is time to move on to the true reason I am speaking this evening. I shall bid you a humble adieu."

Laken bowed. Queen Perpetua nodded and smiled. She gave Tremble a slight wink. Tremble could almost feel it in her heart.

"Wait, can you please tell me why your voice sounds so familiar to me?"

Tremble took a step back toward the window. The older woman looked straight at Tremble and smiled.

"It is because when you were a baby, I sang to you in your dreams."

"Why? I mean, I don't understand."

"My darling granddaughter, Jasmine, cried every night after she left you. If I had not sung, you would have heard her cries. You would have remembered the sound of her crying. I sang to her. I sang to you."

Tremble glanced at Dana. Her face was wet with tears. Tremble could not compose the words to communicate her feelings.

"Thank you, Queen Perpetua."

"Grandmama will do just fine, my dear."

Before King Baldric could utter another word, the window turned black. Dana jumped up and pulled Tremble into a hug.

"I believe we should take a break, Laken." CeCe rose from

the couch. "Let's go outside and take a walk."

Once they were alone, Tremble let her feelings out. "Oh, Mom, what are we going to do? I don't like any of this. I can't help but feel sorry for Jasmine, but I don't want to learn anymore."

"Tremble, this is too much for anyone to take in such a short time. Your father and I knew little of what we are now hearing. But, you cannot deny your heritage. We have been able to protect you thus far. But, we cannot protect you from your destiny. You must call upon that power within you now. We must remain confident in those that your mother has sent to us. I will be with you every step that I am able to be. I will forever be holding you in my heart."

Chapter
Seven

"AS TIME PASSED, there became divisions among the territory that we know as Neverwrong. While all the sisters were able to rule together peaceably, it was difficult for them to keep Baldric in check. The average citizens of our land knew little of this division, but those who were in service to the Royal Family, such as positions that CeCe and Bridget hold, knew of the problems."

Laken, CeCe, and Bridget had returned from their walk. They were all back in the living room listening to Laken.

"As hard as the sisters tried to keep the peace, there seemed to be an undercurrent of friction that no one wanted to talk about. Time passed. The Seven visited other magical kingdoms and found mates in the families who lived there. All returned to Neverwrong and began their adult lives. They had children and grandchildren and ruled peacefully. The commoners of Neverwrong were bestowed with unique skills and magical powers. It was the sisters who had decided to share magic with those of their kingdom. Neverwrong grew in population and prosperity. It was divided into a city and several villages. Queen Perpetua ruled over the central city. King Baldric had domain over a vast expanse of countryside with large farms. The other five sisters each ruled over a village. Over time, their rule passed to daughters or sons. Baldric and his descendants only had sons. This pattern began early on. The first born of each generation descended from Baldric has been male. That is, until now."

Silence engulfed the room.

"You mean?"

"Yes, Tremble. The current ruling descendant of King Baldric is King Marcus. He is your grandfather. Your father is his firstborn, his only child."

"And I am his firstborn."

Tremble stood up and walked toward the window. The view had returned to the lovely neighborhood where she had grown up.

"It has always been that the first born descendant of Queen Perpetua is the Supreme Ruler. Now, for the first time in our history, the heir is also a direct descendant of King Baldric. This was prophesied at the beginning of our time." CeCe had joined the conversation.

"But, can't I just abdicate or whatever the right word is?"

"It's not that simple. The prophecy that foretold your birth is very clear that two lines of the family would unite. The heir, you, is the fulfillment of the prophecy and the one who is being sought by the evil force. Actually, it does not matter whether you rule or not. What matters is that you exist. You would not really be considered a ruling heir until your twenty-first birthday."

"Unless—" Bridget chimed into CeCe's explanation.

"Unless, both of your parents had passed before then. It is one of the reasons that we think that at least one of your parents is still alive. Queen Perpetua, even in her present state, is still the one who announces a new ruler. She would know when the reign of power would need to pass from one generation to the next."

As CeCe was talking, Laken again used the window to allow them to see into another world and another time.

"It's like watching a movie." Dana commented, as before them a beautiful wedding ceremony appeared. "Oh, how beautiful Jasmine is."

The view changed to the interior of a huge castle, but it was also a lush, tropical garden at the same time. This time, it became three-dimensional and they had the feeling that they were walking around in the courtyard with the other wedding guests.

"It is so hard to get past the differences in color. It's all I can see."

Tremble went up to the window. Now that she knew she could, she had a strong desire to step right into the scene. She didn't want to scare her mother again.

"Yes, the colors of our world are quite different than what we experience here." Bridget's voice seemed to be coming from above. "But, both worlds can be very lush and beautiful. It is a shame that humans have destroyed so much of the beauty of their environment."

Tremble turned and saw that Bridget was indeed floating. Her head was almost touching the ceiling.

"Ah, Bridget, are you okay?"

Everyone turned and looked in her direction.

"Get down from there."

CeCe's voice made Bridget realize that she was floating. She eased back down to the floor, smiling.

"Excuse me. I'm very sorry. I seem to lose my bearings when I see these beautiful views of my homeland."

"As I was saying," Laken continued. "There was a royal celebration for the wedding of Jasmine and Forrest. King Marcus rarely came to such formal family gatherings. It seemed that even centuries later, King Baldric's descendants still hung on to his temperament. All of them, until your father came along; I am told that King Forrest is very different." Laken paused and looked at Tremble. His gaze was so strong that she had to look away. "Like Baldric, King Marcus had a jealousy toward the other families and all that they represented. By this point, several generations and a couple of hundred years had passed since the original seven siblings had formed their kingdoms. Some of the extended family had not met King Marcus." Laken turned back toward the window. "As you can see, there was a large crowd in attendance."

Tremble's eyes were focused on the bride and groom. This beautiful woman had given birth to her. This handsome man was her father. She saw all of her features in the two of them. She saw herself in these strangers.

"They look very happy."

"Oh, they were. It was a glorious day." Bridget's voice, ground level now, rose up from the corner of the room. She had placed her chair in the corner. "It gives me a wall on each side to help keep me grounded."

"You were there, Bridget? It hadn't occurred to me that you might actually know them." Tremble smiled.

"Oh, yes, CeCe was also. We worked for your grandmother. Queen Eliza was a wonderful woman."

"Was? She is deceased?"

"Yes, an equally tragic story for another day. Her death is

what made way for your mother to take the throne. It was shortly after this beautiful celebration."

Tremble focused back on her parents. Their attire reminded her of a medieval story. The silk and jewels that were covering her mother were breathtaking. Instead of the traditional white that most brides wore in Tremble's world, her mother's dress was layers of all the beautiful colors of jewels. The contrast was striking; yet, it was simplistic at the same time.

"Her dress is beautiful."

"The gown was designed and handmade by the woman who raised your father."

With a whirl of Laken's hand, another scene came into view. A small woman was kneeling next to Jasmine. She was sewing beads onto the wedding dress.

"This is Marina. She is the servant who raised your father."

"What happened to his mother?"

Tremble was beginning to feel like she was learning new characters in a soap opera. Tremble laughed.

"Why are you laughing?"

Tremble's reaction had not escaped Laken's notice. All eyes turned to her.

"Well, I, it just seems like this is all like a soap opera."

"I'm sorry, I do not understand that term." Laken looked at CeCe and Bridget.

"Allow me." Bridget stood up and turned on the television screen. She quickly flipped through several channels. "This is a soap opera, Laken. It is a television show created by humans. There is a continuing story line and everything that occurs is rather melodramatic."

Laken stared at the screen and listened to the conversation of a particular scene.

"I'm not sure that I understand the comparison."

"Never mind, we ladies do. Yes, Tremble, this story will have moments that you will find very similar. Unfortunately, it is not a fictional tale."

Bridget turned the TV off and sat back down as she motioned for Laken to continue.

"As I mentioned before, King Marcus was not the most pleasant of men. I suppose that we may never know for certain, but there is reason to believe that King Marcus was responsible for the demise of his wife, Forrest's mother."

"The demise? This story keeps getting better and better."

"Demise is the only word that I feel is appropriate. We are not sure what happened to Queen Esmeralda. She simply disappeared."

"What Laken does not want to say is that Queen Esmeralda escaped the grips of King Marcus. It has long been thought she resides here in the human world." CeCe watched as shocked expressions crossed both Tremble and Dana's faces. "Do not be afraid. She disappeared long before Tremble was born. It was actually her seamless disappearance into this world that may have prompted Jasmine to hide you here. Belladonna has alluded to that."

"She is my grandmother, is that right?" Tremble looked at Laken. He nodded. "You're telling me that my grandmother is hiding out in this world."

"That is not for certain." Laken was glaring at CeCe.

"Oh, stop it, Laken. It is for certain that Esmeralda, at least, at one point was." CeCe shook her head and turned toward Tremble. "We will not get into it at the moment, but your grandmother was famous in this world for a brief period of time. She didn't set out to be, but it happened nonetheless. She disappeared shortly thereafter. Bridget will tell you the story later.

Tremble glanced at Bridget. She was eating another cinnamon roll, but she looked up and gave Tremble a wink.

"As I was saying, Marina was a servant. She was married to the chief manservant of the royal court. His name was Reynolds. He was the closest companion of Jasmine's father, your grandfather, King Jonathan. She was also very close to Queen Eliza, she was your grandmother."

"Okay, I'm confused. Queen Eliza was Jasmine's mother and King Jonathan was her father. Which one is a descendant of Queen Perpetua?"

"Queen Eliza."

"It's all rather confusing." Tremble began to rub her forehead.

"My dear, Tremble. We have only just begun."

Morning turned into afternoon. Everyone was beginning to look tired. CeCe took a long drink of the lemonade that Dana had made. They had ordered a couple of pizzas and only a few pieces remained. Everyone looked a little sleepy. Laken resumed with the story.

"It was on the day of your parents' wedding that everything began to change. It began to become clear to many that Jasmine and Forrest would be the key to the fulfilling of the prophecy." Laken knelt down in front of Tremble. "It was the beginning of why we are all here. The prophecy had already foretold of your birth. It did not foretell your name or the names of your parents. But, it was the first time that anyone from any of the family lines had married."

"Everyone keeps mentioning this prophecy thing. Are you ever going to tell me what the prophecy says? Does it tell what is going to happen to me?"

The three looked at each other.

"I'll take this one, Laken."

CeCe stood up and walked to the window. She had her back to everyone else, so it was hard to see what she was doing. She whispered something, and then the view from the window instantly changed. They could see a beautiful city. It was all colors with the busy movement that any Earthly city would have.

"This is the capital city of Neverwrong. It is called Tristeza. It is an ancient word meaning sorrow."

"Sorrow? Is there something I should know about here?"

"The name was chosen by Perpetua. It is said that she never revealed to her subjects her reasons for the name. It will soon become apparent to you why she did so." Laken looked at the others before he resumed. "This is how the city looks today. When we speak of the prophecy, it was given to us by a man named Meserve. He is one of the wisest beings to have ever lived. He is also one of the oldest. He knows of the force that destines to destroy the Royal Family of Neverwrong."

"I don't understand."

"Meserve prophesied regarding the events leading up to your birth and some of the things that would occur thereafter. He told of the letter being revealed." CeCe paused and looked at Bridget.

"You must tell her."

"Belladonna said no." Laken was back in the conversation. His voice was strong. Tremble saw his square jaw was clinched.

"This child possesses free will. Belladonna does not have the power to interfere with that."

"But, you know what her decision will be if she hears it."

"No, I do not."

"Will you all please stop talking about me as if I am not here? Tell me, CeCe."

"The prophecy says that you will not go to the Kingdom of Neverwrong."

"Because?"

"It says that the heir will forsake her homeland."

"I don't understand." The image in the window instantly changed. The once beautiful city became a desolate wasteland. An ugly yellow hue hung over it, like a covering. There were no signs of life.

"Tremble, this is what the prophecy says Neverwrong will become after the heir forsakes her homeland."

Tremble hears Laken's words, yet she cannot connect them with what she is seeing.

"Who does this?"

"The evil force vows to destroy Neverwrong." Bridget spoke from the corner where she still sat. "He pledges to destroy the kingdom and all those who inhabit it."

"How can this be stopped?" Tremble's question met silence. "Come on, tell me."

"You are the only one who can stop this. You must face the evil that wishes to destroy you."

Bridget's voice did not float. It slapped Tremble in the face.

Tremble went upstairs to her old room to lie down for a while, but she was too restless to sleep. She quietly crept to the top of the stairs and listened to what the others were discussing. She thought that perhaps they might reveal something while she was out of the room that might be beneficial for her to know. Even though she couldn't see him, she could sense from the sound of Laken's voice that he was pacing the floor.

"I don't think we should have told her."

"She has a right to know." Bridget's normally cheerful voice was replaced with one that was serious. "This is her destiny. She cannot deny it."

"Now, she has a choice to make. Her Highness did not want her to have any options."

"Belladonna does not know this child. We do." Bridget's voice was gaining more edge. "I know that she will do the right thing. Dana and Andrew taught her to do what was right."

"Right for who?"

Dana's voice sounded tired. It reminded Tremble of the final week of her father's life.

"I miss you, Dad. I really need you now." Tremble whispered and leaned her head against the stair rail.

"Dana, I know that all this must be frightening for you, but—" CeCe said.

"But, what? Were you entrusted with her life from the moment she was born? Have you spent every single day of her life loving and caring for her? Did the evil cancer take away the only other person in the world who understood what your precious daughter's life meant to you?"

"Dana, we don't presume to know—"

"Presumption is the only thing that any of you know. The only person, and I mean the *only* person, who understands what I am going through is Jasmine. How I wish that she were here now. I cannot make this decision."

"Dana, with all due respect, it's not your decision to make.

It's Tremble's." Laken's voice was steady, but there was an undertone of fear.

"I want to meet Belladonna."

All eyes turned to where Tremble stood in the doorway.

"Tremble, you are not allowed to go to Neverwrong without Belladonna's permission. I am the only one authorized to take you there."

"Okay, Mr. Protector, but can't you bring her up in the window? I mean, I've met dead relatives today, surely you can conjure up a live one."

"Yes, I guess that would be possible."

CeCe stood up and walked toward Tremble. "I know that you must feel like we have betrayed you, but, my dear, we have done all of this out of love. Love for you, love for Jasmine, love for our homeland."

"We were amazed at your natural talent for advertising. You earned the internship, fair and square." Bridget's voice had once again begun to float. "We really never dreamed that you would love it so much."

"You are both very good at what you do." Tremble paused. "Bridget, did you ever have a husband?"

"No, that would have been too complicated. But, I did create my dream one, my dream human."

Bridget's response made Tremble sad. She wondered if she would ever have any real love in her life.

"Mom, was Jake real?"

"What do you mean, Tremble?"

"Was he really my boyfriend?"

"Yes, as far as I know, he is a real human boy."

Her mother's comment made her think of all the many times they had watched *Pinocchio* as a family. Her father's jokes that the character would be as close as Tremble would get to a real boy while he was around.

"Why did Jake leave? Why did he all of a sudden decide to go into the military when he had never discussed it before?" They all looked at each other and down at the floor. "Great! I might as well go to Neverwrong. I don't stand a chance of having a life here." Tremble turned to leave, but stopped. "Laken, you contact Belladonna. I want to talk to her before the day is over."

"Tremble, I am not sure—"

"I SAID contact her. I am the heir of Neverwrong. YOU can start treating me that way."

TREMBLE REMAINED IN her room for the rest of the afternoon. She spent most of the time with a pillow clutched to her chest as she gazed out of her window. Choo Choo stayed by her side.

She'd almost forgotten about her cell phone until she heard it ringing. She had not remembered that she had brought it up-stairs when she came to her room earlier. A glance at the screen told her it was Jake. It had been so long since he had called her that she had to stare at his name for it to register. It surprised her that she had not deleted his number.

"Hello."

"Hey, I was afraid that maybe you had changed your num-ber." Jake paused, but Tremble remained silent. "Listen, I'm re-ally sorry that I surprised you like that yesterday. Maybe I should have called you first. But, I was afraid that you might not see me if I asked permission."

Tremble thought for a moment considering what she would have done.

"What do you want, Jake?"

"I wanted to say that I'm sorry. And, you looked beautiful."

"Okay, thank you."

"Tremble, I never meant to hurt you. Really, it's the last thing I wanted to do. I am not sure why I enlisted so quickly. It just seemed to hit me that it was the thing to do. I mean, I'm doing okay in it and all; I am a little surprised that I did it."

Tremble couldn't help but feel a little sorry for him. Based on what she knew now, it was likely that his behavior was not completely his fault.

"I was wondering if you might consider having dinner one night before I have to return to duty?"

As Jake was finishing his sentence, Tremble heard a soft knock at her door and saw her mother peek in. "Tremble, may I come in?"

Tremble motioned for her to enter as she spoke to Jake. "I am kind of busy right now. Maybe we can talk later."

Jake was silent for a moment before he continued. "Okay, I understand. You probably have a whole other life without me now."

"You have no idea how true that is. You take care."

As Tremble clicked the 'end' button, she looked down at her screen to see a text message from her friend, VeVette. 'Hey, where u been? Going 2 beach with fam. B back Sun. Text me.' For a moment, Tremble wondered if VeVe was someone who had been placed into her life. But, everything in her heart said no. They had been friends since kindergarten. If there was one thing that Tremble knew for a certainty, it was that VeVe couldn't keep a secret. She would never have been able to keep from Tremble such an incredible story. The thought made her sad, as she knew that she could not tell her dearest friend what she had just learned.

Tremble looked up to find Dana sitting in the big papasan chair across the room. The young, beautiful mother who Tremble loved appeared to have aged twenty years now. The soft lines on her forehead, which might have yesterday been considered as coming from laughter, now appeared as deep crevices of worry and sadness. Again, this change reminded Tremble of the passing of her father, the day his big bright light left their lives.

"Darling, I'm sorry that we weren't more truthful with you. I swear it is the only thing we ever did like that. Remember, how we never told you that Santa was real or the Easter Bunny? We thought that at least we could be honest about everything else since there was so much deceit we seemed to be hiding."

"Yes, the other parents hated you because I stood up in kindergarten and revealed that Santa was a fake in show and tell."

"It was the only time that your father and I were sent to the principal's office. I thought we were going to be tried for being un-American." Dana chuckled and was lost in thought for a moment. "It made us sad because no one came to your birthday party a few months later."

"No one except for VeVe."

"Yes, VeVe's parents were fine with it."

"Mom, they aren't—"

"Oh no, no connection whatsoever."

"That's a relief."

"VeVe is your true, blue friend. Don't have any doubts about that. You realize that you can't tell her about this, at least not now."

"Yes, I am afraid that I will have to make up some wild story, if I go away."

"Oh, I don't want to hear this go away talk. You don't need

to go off and fight someone else's battles. You belong here."

"I know, Mom, but you saw the picture. I can't just ignore that. It would be like seeing someone hurt on the side of the road. You have to do something."

"Sure. You go find help and send it back to them."

"We know very little about this whole Neverwrong situation, but it seems pretty clear that I can't send someone in my place."

Tremble stretched out on her bed and patted the space beside her for her mother to do the same. Dana moved to the bed, and stretched out. They both gazed at the ceiling.

"Remember the year that Dad painted the ceiling black and put all those glow-in-the-dark planets up?"

"Yes, a black ceiling was extreme, even for an eight-year-old. Your father had some imagination."

"I remember he and I laid right here, just like we are now, and he was naming off all of the planets and stars for me." Tremble paused as she felt her mother take hold of her hand. "You know, I also remember that he had placed one big star over there in the corner and said it was my own personal star that I could fly away to one day." Tremble sat up and looked back at her mother. "Do you think it was his way of telling me something?"

"I don't know. He didn't like it that we couldn't tell you. He thought that one day you would hate us for all that we kept from you. I didn't agree."

"I don't hate you. It's all very overwhelming. It probably would have been worse if I heard this when I was a child."

"Yes. Do you remember the time that we made that last minute Christmas trip to New York City?"

"Absolutely, that was the coolest trip. I think I was twelve."

"Yes, well, we took that last minute trip because we were notified that there might be danger. We never actually found out if it was true or not. If you remember, when we returned home, the Garlands were gone."

"Oh, wow, I had forgotten that. Why did we go to New York City?"

"It's a huge city. You can get lost there. It's hard to find someone in a crowd. We thought that it might be the safest place. We had no idea what kind of power those who were after you possessed, but we thought it would be harder for them to harm you in front of an audience." Dana sat up and rose off the bed. "You come back downstairs when you feel like it. I have some dinner in the oven. The three of them have gone to talk to Belladonna."

"I wonder how they are doing that."

"Who knows, but I bet it is a long distance call."

Tremble laughed. Her mother still had her sense of humor. "I love you, Mom."

"I love you more."

FIVE PEOPLE SAT around the dinner table that evening and they all pushed their food around their plates.

"Lovely dinner, Dana." Bridget was cheerful. "Polynesian chicken is delightful."

"I love the assortment of steamed veggies." CeCe was monotone. "The herbs you have added are very aromatic."

"I like the rolls. They taste sweet."

Laken must have learned polite dinner manners at Protector School. Tremble smirked to herself.

"Will everyone please stop talking about the food and tell me what I want to know?"

"We can contact Her Highness whenever you are ready.

She is prepared to talk to you." Laken wiped the corners of his mouth with his napkin.

"Then, I suggest everyone eat up and let's get on with this."

"Tremble, there are a few things that we need to tell you first." CeCe set down her water glass. "Belladonna is the only member of her family still in Neverwrong. As we told you, the whereabouts of your mother, Queen Jasmine, are not known. Belladonna had contact with her during the early years of your life. But, as the years have passed, the contact has ceased. Their parents, your grandparents, died a number of years ago. Belladonna is in royalty limbo, you might say. She is not the Queen, but she has been forced to rule. It has been a difficult predicament for her."

"I'm not sure how I am supposed to respond to that." Tremble glanced at Dana.

"No one is expecting you to, my dear." Seated next to Tremble, Bridget touched her hand. "We just want you to understand that you might feel some hostility from Belladonna. She is under a lot of stress."

"Does she want to be Queen?"

"No, she does not." Laken was very forceful with his answer. "She is very devoted to Queen Jasmine. She has overseen your protection almost your entire life. I was personally trained by her." Laken paused and looked at CeCe, who nodded. "But, she, like many, would like for this matter to be over. She would like to have her sister back. She would like to have her own life."

"Well, let's go talk to her then."

A BEAUTIFUL SHADE of teal came into view as Laken opened the drapes. It looked as if they were viewing a very long hallway. There were doors on each side. Golden doorknobs glistened and sparkled. Down at the end, one of the doors slowly opened and a figure appeared.

"Here she comes."

CeCe and Bridget rose and stood at attention. Dana and Tremble looked at each other and followed their lead. They watched as the figure came closer and closer. The brightness glowing from the doorknobs made it hard to see her face, at first. She was silhouetted in a fog, the color of fuchsia. She glided down the hallway like a model on a runway with every bit as much confidence and grace.

"Good evening, Laken."

Now in full view, the woman was in a word—gorgeous. Tremble had seen the dark-featured beauty of Jasmine, but this woman was a light-featured mirror image of her sister.

"Your Highness."

Laken bowed. Belladonna threw the train of her long jacket over the back of a backless chair as she sat down. Her outfit was solid black with multicolored stitching. As she moved, it gave the appearance of a flowing movement.

"May I present those who are with me this evening?" Belladonna nodded. "Chief Guardian CeCe of the Neverwrong Militia, and Assistant Chief Guardian Bridget of the Neverwrong Intelligence Bureau." Both bowed.

"Ladies, it is wonderful to see you again. I appreciate your loyal service these many years."

"Your Highness, it has been our distinct honor." CeCe replied. "We would have not wanted any other assignment."

"Your Highness, I shall now present Ms. Dana Dawson."

Dana nodded and was about to speak.

"There are no words to fully express my family's gratitude for the years that you and your late husband devoted to taking such wonderful care of my sister's daughter."

The hairs on the back of Tremble's neck rose as she listened to Belladonna's words.

"I'm sorry, but we have loved and raised Jasmine's daughter as our own child. We are the ones who have been grateful to Jasmine for giving us her daughter."

There was deafening silence.

"Forgive me; my comment did not give the proper emphasis to the role that you have so lovingly fulfilled. If Jasmine was here, she could more properly convey the deep appreciation we—"

"If Jasmine was here, we wouldn't be having this conversation." Tremble interrupted Belladonna. "Jasmine gave me to Dana and Andrew Dawson. I became their daughter and theirs alone. I know that she did this out of love and concern for my safety and I appreciate that. But, let's not get into any battles over who is my family."

"Tremble, you should not speak—"

"No, no, Laken. It is fine. Tremble has the right to show loyalty to the Dawsons." Belladonna paused as she directed her attention to the area where Tremble was standing. It was just out of her view. "Tremble, my darling niece, could you please come closer so that I may see you?" Tremble did as she was asked. "Ah, yes, I am very pleased to finally meet you. I see the beauty of all of your parents in your aura—my beautiful sister Jasmine and her dear husband Forrest and the unconditional love that was given to you by Dana and Andrew."

"Your Highness."

Tremble tried to restrain the irritation she felt. She must not let her frustration with the situation cloud the meeting. Under other circumstances, the introduction to an aunt would be a welcomed experience.

"Oh, my dear, you must call me Aunt Belladonna." She paused and adjusted a beautiful amulet that hung around her neck.

"Aunt Belladonna, I have never had an aunt before. That necklace is amazing. Is it a family heirloom?"

"Well, my dear, I have had a niece for over twenty years. I have missed being able to be a known part of her life. Our relationship shall be as precious and rare as the jewel that adorns my neck. You are correct. This necklace belonged to Queen Perpetua. We are told it was worn by her mother at the birth of each of her children. This actually now belongs to Jasmine, but I am wearing it for safe keeping."

Belladonna fingered the stone before she patted it and returned her gaze to Tremble.

"It looks like a ruby." Tremble heard Dana speak behind her.

"Many have mistaken it for that. It is an even rarer jewel than that. This center stone is twenty-one carats of red diamond. It is the rarest of diamonds in all the universe."

"Your Highness, I believe that Tremble would like to hear more about how the situation we face came to be." Laken gave a side-glance to Tremble.

"Yes, I would like to know why I have been in danger. I would also like to know about the whereabouts of Jasmine and Forrest."

Tremble sat down in a chair that Laken had placed in front of the window. It made it appear as if Tremble and Belladonna were sitting across a table from one another.

"That is a long story indeed, and one that will take some explaining from your friends there for you to thoroughly understand. But, a short version would begin at your parents' wedding. Jasmine was the fairest of all of the princesses of the extended Royal Family of Neverwrong. It was not a popular thing for her to marry, well, what some might say was, a distant cousin. It was thought that this would only increase the power that our particular line of the family held."

"Those who descended from Perpetua."

Belladonna raised an eyebrow. "Yes. It appears that your guardians have already begun teaching you about our world." Belladonna paused and looked at the others. "Jasmine had many suitors from neighboring kingdoms. But, from a very young age, she only had eyes for Forrest. He was indeed her true love."

"Was?" Tremble looked intently at her aunt.

"I do not know either of their whereabouts, Tremble. I know that Jasmine has increased the wall of invisibility now to the point that I cannot penetrate it. That tells me that she is alive. She could not maintain that level of spell if she was in captivity or not living. After your fourteenth birthday, we met in the Gardens of Tranquility for two days. She had become very weak from all of the constant power that she had invested in the spells around you. I think that Dana may be aware of this, but you came into the first serious phase of your powers as you fully came into puberty around that time. Because of this, Jasmine was able to align some of your powers to help you begin to protect yourself."

"Was that the night that I had those amazing dreams about Jasmine?" Dana sat down on the couch behind Tremble.

"Yes, that was the night." Belladonna gave Dana a huge smile. Her teeth glimmered like diamonds. "Only it was not a dream. Jasmine was in your home that evening. It is the only time that she ventured back. I was there as well, but I was stationed on your roof."

"The dream was so real, so vivid. Andrew couldn't believe how detailed." Dana paused, thinking back to that night. "Andrew was working at the hospital that night. Would he have had the dream as well, if he were home?"

"I cannot say for a certainty, but I do believe that Jasmine wanted specifically to communicate with you as she increased Tremble's powers. She wanted you, in some way, to understand what was happening and help her."

"I did. I didn't grasp that at the time. But, now, I see it clearly."

"I don't understand. Wasn't I just going through regular human puberty?" Tremble turned around and looked at her mother.

"It would have seemed so to you, as your girlfriends were going through changes as well. Someone can correct me, but the biology appears to be basically the same. I noticed glimmers of your powers and unique skills then. I tried to downplay them. It was around that time that I noticed you could describe the taste of something before you ate it."

"Huh? Can't everyone do that?"

"I would say that humans could do that if they have tasted the food before and it is in their taste memory. The brain has logged the flavors and filed them away with the aromas." Bridget spoke up. "For humans, there is not that connection if you haven't already had the taste experience."

"Exactly." Dana continued her story. "We were at an Indian restaurant one night. Remember when Dr. Patel invited us to his family celebration when his parents visited from India?"

"Oh, yes, my introduction to Indian food. I loved it."

"You most certainly did. I was glad that the Patels were so occupied with their family conversations, because you described how your curry chicken tasted before you took the first bite."

"Hmmm, I never realized that." Tremble turned back to face Belladonna.

"Humans expect their senses to be separate. Our talents tell us otherwise. Actually, humans could combine senses as well, if they would just take the time to practice and become intuitive into themselves." Belladonna looked off to the side again. This time, she spoke to whoever interrupted her. "That's impossible. I specifically told him not to—" Tremble noticed how quickly Belladonna's anger could arise. She seemed, for a split second, to forget that she had an audience. "I am sorry, but I must end our conversation. There are urgent matters that I must address. Tremble, it has been a pleasure speaking with you and Dana."

As if on cue, Laken, CeCe, and Bridget walked closer to the window. "Do you have instructions for us, Your Highness?" Laken seemed eager.

"I have many things to discuss with the three of you, but negligence on the part of others prevents me from doing that." Belladonna paused. Tremble watched as again her aunt fingered the stone of the amulet. Touching it seemed to calm her. "For now, I would like for CeCe and Bridget to take a few days off and rejuvenate their powers. This is very important." They both nodded, seeming to understand Belladonna's unspoken meaning. "Laken, I wish for you to continue to educate Tremble about Neverwrong and our history, as it applies to our mission. Also, please begin showing her how to use some of her elementary powers. I do not want her causing any harm. I must go. Good-night. May all your auras remain safe until we meet again."

Belladonna rose. As she did, the tail of her jacket again swirled behind her dramatically. Tremble wondered if all the queens and princesses portrayed in Hollywood learned that move from real royalty from another world. Like the blink of an eye, the window went blank and Belladonna was gone. Laken quickly pulled the drapes to their closed position.

"I feel like I am in a virtual reality movie. It's a fantasy series called Tremble's Mixed Up Life." Tremble wasn't smiling. She felt even more troubled.

"Worry lines make you old before you time." Dana rubbed her hand over her daughter's forehead.

"Well, perhaps, Laken here will teach me how to remove them." Tremble stood up and released a big sigh. "That was interesting. Belladonna isn't the comforting sort, is she?"

"The weight of responsibility that she has had would overtake someone with less strength. She was not yet an adult when you were born." CeCe answered Tremble. "These last twenty years have been filled with hard decisions and, in many respects, solitude. She has not had what some would consider a normal life for a person of royalty."

Dana looked at the other three in the room. "Belladonna leaving the conversation abruptly seemed to indicate something serious."

"Neverwrong has been in a state of unrest for the last few years. Too much time has passed without our ruler being visible. It has created an undertone of fear. Our magical neighbors have noticed this as well." CeCe made a map appear. It showed the Kingdom of Neverwrong as well as the lands around it.

"What would have to happen for Belladonna to gain the throne?"

"In order for her to become Supreme Ruler, both you and your mother would have to be gone."

"Dead?"

"Unable or unwilling to rule." CeCe made the map disappear.

"I am so grateful that you are here with us to help Tremble

learn these things. It is very overwhelming. But, I know that we can count on your help. Now, I think that we should all take Belladonna's advice and get some real rest."

"This is correct, Dana. We have a long road ahead. You and Tremble both have much to learn. Let us all take a couple of days to recuperate. Can we meet here on Sunday morning and begin teaching Tremble?" CeCe looked around and everyone nodded. "Laken, you will stay with Bridget and me. We have a large home."

"They have a mansion, Laken." Tremble smiled. "The owners of Kaleidoscope Advertising have a home befitting their status in the business world. I am just a lowly intern, but I have been told that their parties are theatrical productions with only A-list attendees."

"And, just how do you know all of this information, lowly intern?" CeCe laughed and shook her head as they all began to walk toward the door.

"My first week at the agency, I made friends with Jillian. I eat lunch with her several times a week."

"Cottage cheese and pineapple." Bridget and CeCe said in union.

"Yes, it's lovely. I have a cheeseburger on the way home. Then, I eat dinner."

"Good night, dear girl." CeCe hugged Tremble. "Have a drink, Dana." She smiled as she hugged her.

AFTER THE OTHERS left, Dana and Tremble sat in the kitchen and stared off into space. They were tired. Tremble felt she had been up for days.

"My life is never going to be the same, is it?"

"Tremble, all your life, we have been protecting you from something. Whether it was scraped knees, hurt feelings, or evil forces from magic kingdoms." Dana smiled and pushed the hair out of Tremble's eyes. "It was a constant undercurrent in this house, between your father and me. But, really, I don't think we completely grasped the reality of it. Not like I do, right now."

Tremble was quiet for a while. "What do you think Jasmine's life has been like all these years?"

"I think I can answer that with some certainty. I think her life has been miserable. We know that she was separated from the person she loved most in the world before she even had a chance to know her. It is obvious that her love for Forrest is deep and strong, and they seem to have had little or no contact as well. She is probably in constant fear for his wellbeing, yours, and her own. Jasmine has been far away from her family and her homeland. She is all alone."

"She must be an incredible person with great strength. I'd like to meet her. Is that okay that I feel that way?"

"It is more than okay. It is the way it should be. I think that your big heart has room enough for both of us. Through the years, I have seen glimmers of her in you. Little snippets of that selfless person that she most certainly is." Dana breathed in a large sigh. "But, meeting her will come with danger. As much as I have tried to protect you, the time is coming when I will not be able to protect you from yourself. I will not be able to shield you from your destiny."

As they rose to leave the kitchen, they both heard a noise. It sounded like a thump at the door.

"What is that?" Tremble whispered, as her mother came up behind her. Dana quietly opened the hallway closet door and retrieved her husband's baseball bat. She moved in front of her daughter and they slowly turned the corner and looked at the front door. They heard the thump again.

With Dana armed and in her best hitting stance, Tremble slowly looked out the accent window on one side of the door. She leaned back and shook her head as she opened the door.

Laken fell back through the open door with a thud. Dana lowered the baseball bat.

"What is going on, Laken? I want some answers!" Dana's voice made Laken cover his ears.

"I was just hiding outside—

"Hiding outside?" Dana joined the conversation. "Why didn't you tell us you were hiding outside?"

"It is my job as The Protector to always be nearby."

"Then, why don't you just stay inside the house with us?" The veins in Dana's neck were protruding.

"I didn't want to alarm you, and I knew you both were tired."

Dana was about to reply when Tremble came up behind her and embraced her.

"I know, Mom, it doesn't make much sense to me either. Let's just thank Laken for doing his job. I suppose we will have to get used to this."

Dana began to calm down and gave Laken a forced smile.

"We all need rest. Laken, you will stay inside. Let's all go upstairs. I will prepare the guest room for you."

Dana went upstairs as Tremble and Laken lingered in the foyer.

"I realize that everything is happening very fast. It's all very scary, I'm sure. Remember, I am here for you. I will teach you and guide you. I will protect you."

Laken gave Tremble a quick smile. Tremble looked closely at

her new companion. It had only been a short time since his arrival in her life, yet she felt a connection to him—easiness. She had to admit, it could be worse. He was a beautiful companion. Any human girl would be thrilled to be guarded by him. Any human girl, she realized that term no longer applied to her. She shook her head and smirked at the thought.

"Why are you smiling?" Laken's words jolted her back to their present conversation.

"Nothing really. It's amazing how quickly life can change."

"In reality, the changes have been there already. You weren't aware of them."

"I suppose."

"Your room is ready." Dana yelled from upstairs.

"Well, it's time we all get some rest." Tremble began to climb the stairs.

"Tremble."

"Yes." Tremble turned and saw Laken looking up at her.

"I've never been sorry, you know."

"Sorry, for what? I don't understand."

Laken climbed the stairs between him and Tremble until he was standing one step below her. It made their height even. "I've never been sorry that I was assigned to be your Protector."

Tremble felt her heart skip a beat as he said those words. She had no idea how to reply, so she simply turned and walked up the stairs.

Chapter Eight

THE FOLLOWING MORNING, Tremble awakened to Choo Choo licking her hand. "You've been hiding from all the strangers, haven't you? I don't blame you. I'd like to hide, too." It was already ten according to the clock. "I can't believe Mom let me sleep this long." She gave her canine friend a big back scratch before she rose out of bed and headed to the bathroom. She expected to see a disaster when she looked in the mirror. Instead, she saw nothing at all.

"MOM!"

As if she had wings, Dana flew up the stairs. She almost had a head-on collision with Laken who was also rushing to Tremble's aid. Laken was no match for Dana's maternal power, and he was knocked to the floor as she passed him by.

"Tremble. Tremble. What? What?" Dana stopped in her tracks. "Where are you?" Dana looked around the room. She kept colliding with Laken who was doing the same.

It was so comical to see the two of them running into each other that Tremble momentarily forgot why she had yelled.

"I'm in the bathroom. You can't see me. I can't see me."

"Oh my." Laken stood at the doorway and listened

"I don't understand. I can hear your voice. Where are you standing?" Dana had again pushed Laken out of the way. She walked past Tremble and pushed back the shower curtain.

"I'm here at the sink."

Dana looked frightened. "This is not right. This should not be happening. Laken, you've got to stop whatever is happening."

"Jasmine has released Tremble's invisibility powers."

"What?" The simultaneous reaction from Tremble and Dana made Laken take a step back.

"This is her way of continuing to protect you, at least for a little while."

"I don't understand."

"Your power of invisibility has been released."

"Do you possess this power?"

"No, it's Royal magic. Not even all of the Royals can master it. As I understand, both Jasmine and Forrest are especially good at invisibility."

Dana reached out and tried to find her daughter by touch. Tremble gasped as Dana's hand passed right through her. "What?"

"Your hand passed through me. Laken, I don't like this. Can you fix this?"

"I will try to find out." Laken turned to leave the room, but stopped. "I'm sure that we can teach you to come in and out of this state. I think Jasmine wanted us to know that it was time for you to use this power."

"I'm still here." Tremble gazed into the mirror. She only saw her mother standing behind her. Dana looked lost "I'm here and I'm scared."

"THERE ARE ONLY two people who have the power to do this."

By midday, everyone was back in the Dawson living room, in front of the window. Belladonna looked very tired.

"Your mother and your father are the only ones who have the ability to change you."

"So, you are saying that one of my parents was definitely here last night and cast some sort of spell on me."

Tremble was pacing. Since they could not see her, it was as if her voice was quickly moving from place to place. It appeared to be making Belladonna nervous.

"Tremble, could you please sit down or stand still? You are making Her Royal Highness uncomfortable." The calmness in Laken's voice was bordering on annoying.

"She can be uncomfortable right along with me. I am not comfortable in my present state, thank you."

"Let her pace. It is her right. This is a most unusual situation. But, in some ways, perhaps, it is quite revealing." Belladonna turned to listen as a slender man entered their view and whispered to her. "This is good news, in many ways. For it tells us that at least one of your parents is safe. They would not physically have to come to you. They would have to use their powers to set this into motion. Frankly, because of the nature of it, I wonder if it is not the work of their combined powers."

"Why do you say that?"

"When we were all children, we frequently played hide and seek. Jasmine and Forrest were masters of invisibility, even at a young age. I did not master it until I was older. When other royal families would visit Neverwrong, it was a game that Forrest frequently suggested. Jasmine and Forrest may not be physically together. It is very doubtful that they are. They have always had the ability to communicate telepathically. It would take a mighty power to prevent it, and the power would have to know they were communicating."

Once again, someone came to Belladonna. This time it was a stocky man in a long red coat and he gave her a piece of paper. She began to read it.

"Belladonna, if I may explain this to Tremble and Dana." CeCe walked to the window, as Belladonna nodded. "We have already told you that Neverwrong is a parallel universe to Earth. If you visited, you would find that life is very similar to what you experience here. People work, take care of their homes and families, and enjoy entertainment and interaction with others. You might also find that there are people there who would remind you of residents of Earth, but their lives are very different."

"Tremble, here on Earth, you are a teenage girl in an average American family. In Neverwrong, you are a princess." Bridget rejoined the conversation. "Here, someone might be the President, while in Neverwrong, this person might be a commoner. Our two worlds are parallel in time, but different in consequence."

"Does this present any danger?"

"That is a very good question, Dana." Belladonna continued. "It can if there is migration between the two. The only way that someone from Earth can visit one of the Kingdoms is if they are brought here, but many of those from our realm have the power and the means to visit Earth. Occasionally, someone from our realm goes to Earth and becomes a celebrity, in one way or another. They use their powers and talents to gain notoriety. Then, they decide they miss their homeland and they disappear. Your news media makes a big deal out of this type of occurrence."

"Are you trying to say that some of our dead celebrities are now residents of Neverwrong?"

"Let's just say that it is possible that some of Earth's most famous historical figures have gone on to lead much simpler lives elsewhere." CeCe seemed to choose her words carefully.

"I had an astronomy teacher by the name of Earhart. She was very nice." Bridget smiled and winked at Dana.

"What does any of this have to do with me being invisible?"

Belladonna stood up and Tremble noticed that she was dressed in a form-fitting silk pantsuit. It was a cream color with beautiful multi-colored embroidery. Her hair was shaped into a French twist. "I have had enough of hearing a voice without a body. Tremble, please come and stand in front of me." Tremble did as Belladonna said. She noticed that her mother kept trying to see her. "Are you there?"

"Yes."

"Very well."

Tremble watched as Belladonna put her hands in a position similar to one that would be used to type on a keyboard. Tremble was surprised to see that it did look exactly like that movement. Belladonna's fingers were quickly moving as if she was striking invisible keys.

"Invisible to the eye. Missing from the touch. Let your presence rejoin us."

Tremble looked down and saw her pajamas as she heard her mother clap with delight. Before she could turn around, Dana's arms were around her.

"Horrendous bedhead." Belladonna laughed with delight. "Just like your mother."

"Thank you, Aunt Belladonna."

"My pleasure, darling." Belladonna looked past Tremble. "Laken, do you remember the invisibility spell that I taught you?"

"Yes, your Highness. I have committed it to memory."

"Please teach it to Tremble immediately. Make sure that she has a mastery of it both ways. Then, CeCe and Bridget, I would like for you to take Tremble and Dana on a trip. Find a wonderful place to stay and begin to let her explore her powers." Belladonna paused. "Laken, I want you to return to Neverwrong."

"But, your Highness, I am not supposed to leave Tremble. You have always said that—"

"And now, I am saying something different." Her voice was stern. Laken's body language showed controlled defiance. "Dana, I realize that as a mother this is all very troublesome. But, use this time as an opportunity to relax. You have done a wonderful job protecting our girl. Now, we will treat you like a queen. Bridget, you will make all of the arrangements, spare no expense. Give Dana time to take care of what she needs to then leave quickly thereafter."

"What about my internship? I'll be a senior in the fall. I need these credits."

No sooner had the words come out of Tremble's mouth than she realized the futility of them.

"My dear, you shall certainly have an 'A' for your internship." CeCe nodded and laughed. "But, somehow, I doubt that you shall ever return to the university."

"Why not? I like college. I might want to build a career in advertising."

CeCe began to speak again, but Bridget held up her hand. "Tremble, I certainly understand your desire to keep your life here. Earth is truly a wonderful place. Perhaps, once all this is, well, settled, you can come back to Earth and resume your education."

"That is preposterous."

Laken's voice rose to a new level. Tremble was beginning to see a strong young man under his humble attitude.

"Tremble shall be part of Neverwrong royalty. She shall not live the life of a commoner on Earth."

"Jasmine did." Belladonna's voice stifled Laken's words. "She chose to live there, not just to protect her child. She could have waited until the final weeks of her pregnancy to go to Earth. If there had been some way for her to truly hide herself and her child there, she would have stayed on Earth and would have raised Tremble herself. She often told me how much she enjoyed being a nurse. She loved helping people. She loved the beauty of human existence."

Laken remained silent after Belladonna finished speaking. Everyone was silent as all eyes turned toward Tremble. Dana took Tremble's hand.

"You and I have survived many things together. We faced your father's illness and death. It was the worst thing we could imagine. Now, it is time for a new challenge, a new sacrifice. We will hope and plan for something better on the other side of this journey. As we have always taught you, we will dream of something extraordinary."

Tremble studied her mother's face and shook her head. "You have never let me down. As long as you are with me, I will be okay." There was silence in the room. Tremble turned toward Belladonna. "Now, I have to trust you. My mother thinks that it is a wise thing for us to leave here, so I guess I need to as well. I am counting on all of you not to let me down."

Chapter Nine

BELLADONNA HAD GIVEN them their marching orders. Everyone was springing into action. Tremble was heading upstairs to shower and get rid of her 'bedhead,' as her aunt called it while CeCe and Bridget were walking to the door.

"Wherever we go, make sure they allow dogs." Tremble said over her shoulder. "Choo Choo is going with us."

"Tremble, I am not sure that is such a good idea." CeCe stood at the bottom of the stairs as Bridget opened the front door.

"I don't care. I want Choo Choo with me. I realize that she probably won't accompany me when I travel to Neverwrong or any other magical place. While I am still on Earth, she stays with me. Case closed."

CeCe raised an eyebrow at Tremble's final comment. She didn't argue. She simply nodded as she followed Bridget out the door.

"I'm not sure that I like this new defiance you are exercising."

Laken came up behind her as she began to climb the stairs. He looked surprisingly calm and relaxed as he leaned on the banister looking like a magazine model.

"I'm not sure that I like why I am having to become this way. It may be very nonchalant to all of you for these events to finally be playing out."

"I don't think that nonchalant is how you should portray us. I agree that we have had years to prepare for what is now transpiring. We do not, however, treat these duties in a casual or blasé manner."

"That's not what I meant. You are all obviously very devoted."

"Then, what do you mean?"

Tremble turned and faced him. She pondered her words. It was hard to put her feelings into sentences that adequately expressed what she was feeling.

"I have to take a speed course in magic. I feel like I have to learn in twenty days what I should have learned in twenty years. There's so much expected of me. I have to save a kingdom; a place that I can't even wrap my mind around. I've got to have some level of control. Yet, that seems impossible. Without it, I'm not sure that I can rise to this."

"Yes, you can, and you will."

"What makes you so sure? You've been raised to protect someone who doesn't want to be protected. I don't want any of this."

"None of us want this for you."

"I will fail."

"No, you won't. You may falter, but you will not fail."

"Again. What makes you so sure?"

"You're the heir of Neverwrong. Your soul is laced with power. Your magic is itching to get out of you. You're smart, determined, and creative."

Tremble shook her head and turned to continue climbing the stairs.

"Besides, you have the best Protector in the history of the world."

She glanced back at him. Laken was beaming. A light was radiating from his body that could only be termed as luminous.

"How do you do that?"

"What?"

"The light. You are glowing."

"That I cannot control. It's love." Laken bowed his head and walked away.

Tremble felt a sadness overtake her. She was not sure where the feeling originated. There were going to be more aspects to this journey than the obvious ones.

Tremble stood in her father's study. His large mahogany desk sat in the same place it always had. Many of his personal items littered the top—a pencil holder, a stack of sticky notes, medical magazines with dates from several years past, a beautiful bronze framed photo of Dana on their wedding day, a smaller frame made of popsicle sticks with a photo of Tremble with her front teeth missing. The bookcase that once held Andrew's medical books was empty. Dana donated the majority of the volumes it had contained to the library at the local community college. The filing cabinet that was once filled with years of paperwork from his medical practice was empty, too. The room was a shell of what it had once been. Very much like the life that had occupied it. Neither Tremble nor Dana visited the room much, but it was an open space that boded well for the task of the morning. Tremble was trying to learn to disappear.

"Shouldn't I be chanting something?" Tremble listened, as Laken had recounted for her the mind exercise she needed to perform.

"Invisibility is accomplished through concentration and focusing on nothingness."

"Yeah, I don't have much of either. I need a chant."

"Tremble, you are not going to always be able to chant when you need to disappear. You need to be able to do this quietly."

Tremble gave Laken a look of disgust and closed her eyes. She concentrated. She cleared her mind. She focused on the thought of disappearing, being invisible, lightweight, and sheer.

"Excellent."

Tremble opened her eyes and looked down. The only word she could think of to describe what she saw was translucent.

"You are almost there. Bravo. Try again."

Tremble closed her eyes.

"How are we doing in here?" Bridget's cheery voice broke Tremble's concentration. "Oh, my. That is not a good look for you."

Tremble looked down and found that all of her was still visible, except for her middle. She was two halves with nothing in between.

"Might work for bikini weather." Tremble rolled her eyes at Laken's sad attempt at humor. "She's made some progress. It will take a little more time though. She lacks consistency. She can disappear in pieces, but not as a whole."

"She's a creative type, like me." Bridget gave Tremble a smile and a wink. "We need to get on the road soon. Belladonna wants you to be able to do this, in case of emergencies. So, I am going to teach you a trick."

"A trick? There are no tricks to learning spells. It is a complex and intricate process of mind-body synchronization and discipline."

Bridget remained quiet until Laken was finished. "I appreciate your strict adherence to protocol, but there are tricks." She nodded to Tremble.

"How do you know tricks? Do you have the ability to disappear like this?" With open eyes, Laken looked straight ahead. He seemed to be focusing on something far away. Within ten seconds, he was invisible.

"Fine work, Laken. I hate to outdo you. But, I must." Bridget closed her eyes and rocked back and forth. Holding both arms bent and up, she snapped her fingers as she said, "Liquefy." Bridget was instantly invisible.

When Laken came back into view, his mouth was open. Tremble almost jumped out of her skin as she felt Bridget's breath in her ear as the woman whispered Tremble instructions. She followed them precisely and quickly disappeared.

Laken had a scowl on his face. He sighed and shook his head.

"Very well. I give up. I guess the important thing is that she can do it. Can she reappear as quickly?"

Bridget's whispered instructions were simple. Tremble was visible again before Laken finished his question. However, Bridget did not reappear as quickly. They merely heard her voice as she exited the room.

"We need to leave soon, Tremble. Get packing."

"I have to admit it. She's good. While you are gone, get her to teach you to disappear from one spot and reappear in another.

The textbook version of that spell is brutal."

Despite his, sometimes, rigid exterior, Tremble could see that Laken had an easygoing and fun side. She hoped circumstances would allow her to see more of that side in the future.

THEY DIDN'T KNOW where they were going, but Tremble and Dana got into a rental car with CeCe and Bridget later that afternoon. During the morning, Dana ran around town like a white tornado tying up the loose ends of her life.

"I just had to get my haircut." Dana started chattering nervously before they even pulled out of the driveway. "I thought that since Choo Choo was coming along, she deserved a spa treatment, too." The poodle had coral colored bows in her hair to match her trimmed apricot fur. She didn't look happy about the bows. She kept digging at her ears.

"Hey, I would have loved a spa treatment, too."

"I'm sure you would have, darling daughter. Unfortunately you were busy learning to disappear." Dana smiled as she put on her designer sunglasses. "There's a sentence I never expected to say."

"Oh, Dana, you have such a refreshing sense of humor. It is one of the qualities I always enjoyed about you and Andrew. You could see the light side of even the darkest situation. Tremble has the same quality."

"With a side order of sarcasm."

CeCe eyed Tremble in the backseat via the rearview mirror. CeCe was driving the large SUV that had been rented earlier that morning.

"Just a side? I thought that aspect of my personality was

more like a main dish."

Tremble was amazed at the level of familiarity and comfortableness that now existed between her and CeCe and Bridget. A few short days before, they were her bosses. Now, they were her teachers, guardians, and friends.

They drove on, watching the landscape change before them. Bridget's attempts at conversation broke up the monotony of the trip.

"Laken will be travelling back to Neverwrong tonight. He really did not want to go. He is so devoted to his assignment."

"How will he travel? Plane, train, snap of his finger?"

Tremble's comment caused an eye roll from CeCe.

"Tremble, I am not sure that you are ready to learn about that yet." Bridget began to answer.

"No, Bridget, Tremble is curious. She will need to learn about this eventually. It may not be long before she takes her first journey to our realm." CeCe looked directly at Tremble through the mirror. "Do you remember in the Harry Potter movies how the children would travel by train to Hogwarts?" Tremble nodded. "Well, it is a similar experience, only it is by plane. There are gates in all of the major city airports that allow boarding to Neverwrong Airlines. You have to be a native of our kingdoms to be able to see these areas."

"Oh. My. Goodness." Dana interrupted CeCe's description.

"What's the matter, Dana?" Bridget turned around in her front seat to see what was wrong.

"Do you remember the times that we took airplane trips when you were younger?"

Tremble thought for a moment. "When we went to Disney World, we flew to Orlando. And there was that trip to Europe for that medical conference of Dad's."

"On each of those trips, Tremble stood facing this blank wall and just chatted away. We asked her who she was talking to, and she said that there was a pretty lady there who was leading people to their plane."

"Both times, the lady had on a purple butterfly." Tremble smiled, reliving the memory. "She was just beautiful. But, she told me that I needed to go back and sit down and wait with my mother."

"Thank you for flying Neverwrong Air. We'll take you to another world." CeCe and Bridget laughed as they said the line in unison.

"You actually fly on a plane to another world?"

"Well, dear, it's not your average plane, but the concept is still the same." Bridget offered Dana and Tremble cookies that she had purchased at their last stop. "It is a means of fast transportation from this world to that world."

"With all this supposed power you can't just beam yourself there?" Tremble watched as CeCe and Bridget exchanged glances. "What did I say?"

"We cannot." CeCe leaned her head on her left hand and drove with her right. "Your mother could. Your father, also."

"And that would mean?" Tremble leaned up.

"That could be how your invisibility powers were bestowed on you the other night. You no doubt will have an equal or greater ability."

"No way! That's hilarious. I failed driver's ed. Transportation doesn't usually come naturally to me." Tremble slumped back down in the seat, shaking her head.

"You don't have to maneuver a four thousand pound metal machine to be able to travel to Neverwrong. Comparatively speaking, it's a little less complicated. It's all about the power of your mind."

CeCe slowed the car down and exited off of the interstate. The sun would soon be setting.

"How much further?" Dana had not asked where they were going.

"It's about two hours to the coast. We should be there before it gets too dark."

"Tremble, we are going to begin to teach you about your powers." Bridget's tone was unusually solemn. "I realize that much of what we will be sharing with you will initially be beyond your comprehension. But, if you keep your mind open and accepting, I believe that your natural tendencies will help make this process smoother and less confusing. We have watched you. You already unconsciously use some of your powers. Some things are second nature to you."

"I have noticed that as well." Dana joined the conversation. "At first, it scared me. I was afraid that others would pick up on it. Gradually, I came to the conclusion that, in many respects, humans are a very accepting bunch. We tend to overlook the unusualness of others as time passes. The unusual becomes less of a difference and more of a personal trait."

"That's very true, Dana." Bridget looked as the GPS announced the next turn. "You are the daughter of an enchanter and an enchantress—here a more familiar term would be warlock and witch. Humans associate negative attributes with those titles. In Earth's past, people who did not even have powers were burned at the stake because others called them witches. That whole Salem period was an abomination. It was a very disturbing time in Earth history."

"In our realm, everyone has powers—some more than others. Your parents are two of the most powerful beings to have ever existed in our kingdoms. This means that your powers will, no doubt, be amazing." CeCe pulled over at a convenience store. "Don't let that go to your head. You will still need to work to develop your powers and learn how to use them with skill."

THE REMAINDER OF the ride was relatively quiet. Dana dozed a little. Bridget answered Kaleidoscope emails from her smartphone. CeCe seemed lost in thought as she drove the two-lane road to their coastal destination. Tremble gazed out of the window and wondered if her life would ever be the same.

It was almost dark when CeCe stopped the car in the driveway of the rental house. Unlike the houses they had seen on the last mile or so, this one was secluded. An open garage sat under the house making the home appear as if it was on stilts. As they all got out, Tremble gazed up at the three-story structure. She could not make out the color of the siding, but she knew it must be a gray or blue or some other fitting color for an oceanfront property. Every side that she could see appeared to be surrounded by sturdy wooden stairs, rising up higher and higher until they reached the top of the house.

"My reservation says that there should be a lockbox near the backdoor."

Bridget finished reading the message on her phone and climbed the first flight of stairs to the house's rear entrance. Tremble followed her.

"It's so ingenious. They have an electronic lock. You use your phone to gain initial access to the lockbox that holds the key and your reservation packet."

As Bridget worked with her phone to open the box, Tremble

walked around the deck to the front side of the house. The last of the sunset was barely visible on the edge of the horizon, the very wet horizon. The orange reflection glimmered on the surface of the vast ocean.

"I had forgotten how calming the sound of the ocean could be." Dana put her arms around her daughter as she joined Tremble at the railing. "Our trips to the beach were few and far between while you were growing up. We should have come more often."

"Dad was always working."

"Yes, in your early years, he was working hard to build his practice. Truthfully, we were always fearful of taking trips."

"Why is that?"

"Probably because of what happened when you were four."

Tremble hadn't realized that CeCe had joined them.

"What happened?"

Dana smiled and shook her head at CeCe.

"You all were there, weren't you?"

"It was me and another associate. We were assigned to your family during the early years."

"What are you two talking about?"

"Tremble, when you were four, we took a trip to New England. It was in the middle of summer. We boarded a train and took a family adventure." Dana returned her gaze to the ocean. "It was supposed to be a glorious family trip. You, however, were going through a slightly rebellious period."

"Slightly?" CeCe chuckled.

"Well, she was four." Dana shook head and laughed. "I can laugh about it now. It was not funny at all then. You were very much into Mickey Mouse, at the time. More precisely, Minnie. You begged and begged us to take you to Disney World. We thought you were just a little too young. So, we decided to turn a medical conference that your father was speaking at in Boston into an extended trip to Cape Cod. We thought you would enjoy the ocean, playing in the sand, making sandcastles. You had other things on your mind."

"Oh yeah, she certainly did." CeCe sat down in an Adirondack chair nearby.

"We rented a lovely house on the coast. Your father was going to spend the first day with us on the beach. Then, he would drive into Boston for the following two days to attend the conference. The plan was that he would return after that and we would all spend the rest of the week together."

Bridget joined them with a tray of beverages.

"This is a delightful place. We have a fully stocked refrigerator waiting for us. I love special service. What are we talking about?"

"Dana and Andrew's trip to Cape Cod."

"Oh my, that was—"

"Let Dana finish the story."

An understanding look passed between CeCe and Bridget. Tremble wondered just exactly how much the two women knew about her life.

"I dressed you in your favorite swimsuit. It was pink and, of course, it had Minnie Mouse on the front. We packed up our stuff and headed to the beach. Poor Andrew's arms were so full of chairs, bags, and an umbrella, he could barely walk."

Tremble watched, as her mother seemed to be consumed by the memory. A look that was mixed with joy and sadness crossed her face.

"We got down to the beach and were setting up for the morning. I tried to get you interested in digging in the sand with your shovel and pail. You would have no part of it. You kept saying you wanted to go. Your father was very tired and lost his patience a little with your tantrum."

"Tantrum?"

"Yes, there is no other word to accurately describe it. You were in full-blown tantrum stage. He said, 'If you wish hard enough, perhaps it will come true.' You took him seriously. You crossed your arms in front of your chest. You took a deep huffing breath and said, 'I WANT TO GO HOME.' No sooner had the word 'home' left your mouth then you disappeared right before our very eyes."

"Disappeared? I knew how to disappear then? What do you mean? Did I run away?"

"No, Tremble. You disappeared. One second you were standing before us and the next you were gone."

"That's how I first met you."

Tremble turned toward Bridget. She was relaxing in a chair next to CeCe. Bridget sat her drink down in the holder that was made into the armrest.

"I was on one of my first Earth assignments. I was stationed at your home while your family was away. You appeared in the kitchen as I was fixing myself an omelet." Bridget looked at Tremble and smiled. "You looked so cute in your little swimsuit. I made you some Mickey Mouse pancakes."

"How?"

"Oh, it is quite easy. You make a large pancake for the head and two smaller ones attached to it for ears."

"No, not how did you make the pancakes. How did I appear back in our kitchen? I don't remember any of this."

"No, you don't. It was erased from your memory." CeCe stood up and walked toward Tremble.

"It was horribly frightening." Dana rejoined the conversation. "Your father and I were frantic until a lifeguard came up and told us to call home."

"A lifeguard? How long did it take the three of you to come up with this story? This really isn't funny. I don't believe you."

Tremble folded her arms. In a blink, she could see herself on that Cape Cod beach. Her mother and father were with her. She had on a pink Minnie Mouse bathing suit and a scowl on her face. She watched as the deviant little girl yelled her wish to go home. She was immediately in her kitchen and a younger version of Bridget was standing before her. Tremble closed her eyes and shook her head. When she opened them again, she was back on the deck.

"How did you do that?"

"We have ways of proving our point." CeCe returned to her chair and took a long drink from her glass.

"I ran back to the beach house and called back to our home. Bridget answered and said that you were eating pancakes, and when you were finished, she would have you wish your way back to us."

"You ate two plates of pancakes. Amazingly, you didn't even ask who I was. While you were eating, I talked to you about your parents. I told you that I was sure they were worried. You agreed. I told you that you should fold your arms again and say out loud that you wanted to be with your parents. You agreed."

"When I returned to the beach, the lifeguard was gone. Your father was just a mess by that point. He thought it was his fault since he had told you to wish for what you wanted. It wasn't long after that when you reappeared again. You said hello to us, then picked up your pail and shovel, and headed to a big mound of sand nearby."

"I don't remember any of it. But, now that I think about it, I do remember that Daddy had a long talk with me about not wishing for things out loud. That I should only wish in my head."

"Yes, the lifeguard told him that was one of the powers Jasmine had left with you. She thought that if you ever got into serious danger that it was a power you needed to have."

"Who was this lifeguard? An employee of Neverwrong obviously."

"No, Tremble, we are not employees of Neverwrong. We are subjects of Neverwrong under the service of her Royal Highness Princess Belladonna. Employees punch a time clock. Our duty is our life."

Bridget rose from her chair as she finished her statement and walked back into the house.

"I believe I will begin to unpack the car." CeCe rose to follow her.

"CeCe, I'm sorry. I didn't mean anything by that."

"I understand, Tremble. But, you must understand as well. Our lives have been in service to your family. We have sacrificed our own dreams to protect the heir to Neverwrong and all those around her. We do not take it lightly."

CeCe walked around the house toward the direction of the car. Tremble sat down in one of the chairs and held her head in her hands.

"I'm so confused. I don't understand any of this. I know I shouldn't let my temper slip. I should be more respectful. But, I don't want any of this. I want my old life back."

Dana sat down next to Tremble.

"I know. The problem is that I'm afraid your old life was just an extension of this. You didn't know it, but we did. It's a lot for you to grasp. It's just going to take time."

"I hope I have time. Somehow, I'm afraid I will not have enough of it."

Chapter Ten

LIGHT FROM A beautiful sunrise peaked through the curtains in Tremble's room awakening her the following morning. Putting on a pair of running shoes, shorts, and a couple layers of shirts, she quietly walked down the stairs from her top floor room. She grabbed a bottle of water off the counter and drank it as she quickly crunched a protein bar. The smell of freshly brewed coffee told her that someone was up.

Walking out onto the large deck, she saw that it was CeCe. The long slender woman lay on a lounge chair like a sleek feline. A cat drinking coffee, that is. Tremble could see the steam coming from the large mug in CeCe's hands. Her hair was wrapped up in a towel, still wet from a shower. She had on large, dark sunglasses. Tremble smiled. CeCe had always reminded her of someone famous and the look completed that illusion.

"Is there coffee on Neverwrong?"

"No. We do not have caffeine of any sort. I think that's why

I love it so much."

"Forbidden fruit."

"Yes. Also, no one runs there for sport, either. If you run in Neverwrong, it means you are either late or something is chasing you."

"Good to know." Tremble finished stretching. "Do you think there will be breakfast when I return?"

"Well, we have your mother and Bridget here. I think it is a pretty good bet. Come back hungry."

"Don't worry."

Tremble ran down the stairs and followed a path of firmly packed oyster shells to the beach. As she got closer to the ocean, she looked in both directions. To her right, she could see someone, in the distance, walking a dog. To her left, in the direction of the rising sun, there was no one. That was the direction she chose.

It was only on weekends that she ran in the morning. College classes and now early work hours made weekday runs difficult. She had opted instead to volunteer to take an elderly neighbor's two Golden Retrievers on runs two evenings each week. Mrs. Hudson, the landlord, lived on the bottom floor of Tremble's apartment building. Everyone else who lived there was under thirty. All of the rents paid for her lengthy retirement. Mrs. Hudson was a spry eighty-eight, but arthritic knees made walking her dear companions a hardship. Her tenants took turns walking the dogs each day. Tremble had Tuesday and Thursday evenings. With Tremble, Bonnie and Clyde got a real workout.

Tremble thought of her two evening companions as she began to run on the edge of the water. She was glad she remembered to call another neighbor, Gary, and ask him to fill in on the evenings she was to be away. On her weekday runs with her two canine friends, she focused her attention on them for their safety. Her weekend morning runs were a time to clear her head, to give clarity to her busy week. That's what she wanted now. She desperately wanted clarity. She doubted that she would find it.

The sun increased in intensity as she ran toward it. At first, she thought that the light was playing tricks on her eyes. Soon, she realized that her eyes were seeing another place entirely. Magic was already invading her consciousness.

"How was your run, dear?"

Dana was the first person who spoke as Tremble entered the kitchen.

"Energizing. It took me to another world."

Dana did not seem to catch what her daughter said, but it did not escape CeCe's notice. Her brow furrowed and she started to speak, but Tremble put her finger to her lips and nodded. Tremble took in the activity in the kitchen as she poured herself a glass of orange juice. Her mother was scrambling eggs. She could see a pan of sizzling veggies on the stove behind the skillet her mother was using.

"Looks like veggie eggs."

"Yes, indeed. Just as you like them."

"Mom started this when I began school. I really didn't want to eat vegetables of any sort. Mom thought I might be more receptive if they were disguised in eggs and cheese."

"Oh, Dana, someone should have told you that Tremble's taste buds would not automatically enjoy this world's vegetables. We could have done a spell for that."

"That would have been nice info to have, Bridget, when

Tremble was, say, three years old." Dana laughed and continued scrambling. "I figured out my own blend of magic for this problem."

"Now, Mom, you had a little help."

"Yes, that's true. The husband of Andrew's office manager worked for a publishing company. He was actually an editor, and he enjoyed writing children's stories. Andrew convinced him to write a story about a little girl who did not eat her vegetables."

"Ingenious." Bridget smiled as she put a plate of Minnie Mouse pancakes in front of Tremble.

"Oh, Bridget, they look wonderful."

Even though Tremble did not remember eating Bridget's pancakes previously, she appreciated the sentiment. Bridget went back to the griddle to make, what Tremble assumed would be, normal pancakes for the rest of them as Dana continued with the story.

"I believe that Ross was the writer's name. Does that sound right, Tremble?"

"No, it was Russ. Russ Debuss. I think we still have the book."

"You have got to be kidding." CeCe seemed intent on her task of cutting up a honeydew, a cantaloupe, and a container of strawberries. "Someone with the last name of Debuss named their son Russ. That seems cruel."

"Hey, Tremble isn't exactly the most common name on the playground."

"You, my dear, were named by Her Royal Highness. Legend has it that your name came to Jasmine in a dream. Your name carries a level of magic and beauty unlike any other in our world." Bridget was precise with her explanation.

"Then, allow me to begin to learn about this world that gave me such a name."

THE HOUSE BRIDGET rented was quite unique. In addition to the garage area, there were three levels. Tremble had chosen the bedroom on the top floor. Some might describe it as a loft. Her room had windows on all sides. It was open and spacious, with only one door into a room that was a closet and a bathroom combined. The feature that Tremble found most alluring was the window seats that were built-in at each of the four windows. No matter the time of day, you could gaze out onto the horizon and, from three of the views, see the ocean.

Bridget and CeCe had taken the two spacious bedrooms on the second floor. Dana had opted for the ground floor suite, which opened up onto a large private deck. It was from that deck that their discussion began.

"Bridget and I will be giving you a rudimentary course in understanding your powers and how to begin using them." CeCe began the conversation.

"I thought that Jasmine put a spell on my powers to prevent accidental use of them."

"She did. But, the opening of the letter released that spell."

"You mean that I have all my powers now?"

Tremble looked down at herself as if this knowledge might reveal a sudden visible difference.

"No, your powers must be developed. You will master one level at a time."

"So, I am not as powerful as some may have thought I would be."

"Oh, no." Bridget quickly responded. She was sitting in a

corner chair, knitting. "You may have powers as vast as anyone in the history of our kingdom. You must learn to use them though."

"I don't understand. Either I have them or not?"

"Let's use the analogy of a runner, since that is a sport you enjoy."

CeCe rose from her chair and took on the manner of a professor. It appeared that she pulled a screen down from the sky, as one stood before them in midair. Tremble saw a person appear, running slowly down a street.

"When someone decides that he or she will take up running, the person does not run a 5K the first week. Consistent, long-term training is required to build the stamina needed for a race of that length." The view on the screen changed. It appeared that a time lapse occurred as the runner ran faster and for a longer period of time. "Just like this runner, you will have to train to use your powers, building on what you learn."

The screen view changed to flashes of brilliant colors. The shades were so breathtaking that both Dana and Tremble gasped at the sight.

"That is so beautiful. It's more than beautiful. I cannot even find a word to adequately describe it." Dana rose from her chair and walked toward the screen. Upon reaching it, she turned to face the others. "I've dreamed this. Periodically throughout Tremble's life, I have seen this scene in my dreams."

Bridget rose and put her arm around Dana as she led her back to her seat. "Yes, before Belladonna sent me on assignment to your family, she gave me a long personal briefing. I felt as if I knew you, Dana, before I even met you. You are very deeply loved by Jasmine. With no disrespect to your husband, it was you who she chose—mother to mother. The two of you have a strong bond. Jasmine visits you via your dreams. It is how she communicates with you."

"Somehow, I knew that."

"I'm sure that she would love to visit you in person to discuss Tremble and properly thank you."

Tremble watched as Dana seemed lost in thought. She could not read the expression on her mother's face. All of the discussion had made her mind wander to a key question that no one had answered yet

"Why hasn't anyone ever tried to kidnap me?"

Tremble was surprised that Bridget's expression did not change. She responded with the same cool confidence she would use in a business meeting.

"The spell that was put on you to guard you is extremely powerful. It is a feeling spell."

"What does that mean?"

"A feeling spell is one that not only protects, but also has the power to ascertain the intentions of those who come in contact with it. The spell can detect those who intend to harm you by reading the being's thoughts and intentions."

Tremble considered what Bridget had said. She could hear the woman continue to talk to her mother in the background as her mind searched her memory. There was something that happened when she was a teenager.

"Dillon Finney."

"What did you say?" Bridget turned to Tremble.

"Dillon Finney. He was my junior prom date."

"Yes, we remember him."

"You remember him. You weren't around then." Tremble paused. "I forget, you've always been around. Was he someone who was trying to hurt me?"

"I do not think he would have hurt you. But, I am certain

that he would have kidnapped you." CeCe's response was quick and direct.

"What? Why weren't Andrew and I told about this?" A look of concern crossed Dana's face.

"We started to, Dana, until we fully realized that it was Jasmine's spell that had stopped him. Dillon Finney was not a mortal. He was sent here. We learned then that Jasmine's spell was powerful enough to protect Tremble."

"I barely remember Dillon. Did you even go on another date with him besides the prom?"

"No, Mom, I didn't. After we left the prom, Dillon wanted to go for a drive. He actually took me to the airport." Tremble laughed. "Or that's where he tried to go."

"Go ahead and tell your mother." CeCe sat down and the screen disappeared. "It's a very good story."

"We got to the entrance of the airport and the car just stopped. It was still running, everything appeared to be working. It just refused to move one inch forward. Dillon put it in reverse and it moved just fine. He shifted back to drive and got right to the line to enter the airport property and it stopped again. He tried it about four or five times. Then, out of nowhere a policeman appeared, blue lights and all. He took one look at us and told Dillon that he didn't think the prom was at the airport. Dillon finally just backed up and turned the vehicle around and brought me home."

"So the policeman was?" Dana smiled as she asked the question.

"The policeman was actually Anton, who you met as the lifeguard."

"Oh, how wonderful. He was such a nice man."

"He was Laken's father." Bridget's smile turned into a frown.

"Was?" Tremble suspected there was more to the story.

"As Laken told you, he was born on the same day as Tremble. From birth, he was intended to be Tremble's Protector. He came into existence biologically, as all beings do. Only his genetic makeup was influenced by a spell. The process was very similar to what humans once called a test tube baby. A surrogate mother was used. Anton was assigned to raise him. Laken spent months at a time with Belladonna and her closest companions. During those periods, Anton would be assigned to watch over your family. On the night of your prom, Anton's life force was extinguished."

Bridget looked at CeCe. She had moved to the edge of the deck and was looking at the ocean.

"It was a difficult time for all of us. We saw the first glimmer of the dark magic that was the force from which Jasmine was trying to protect you. After that night, we learned the truth." CeCe paused. Her gaze seemed to be seeing far more than the ocean waves. "It is too complicated to try and thoroughly tell you about it now. You need to have a better understanding of our heritage. This force was once connected to the Royal Family. This force intends to gain power over the entire universe. That's the force that killed Anton."

"Laken's father died protecting me?" Tremble began to feel sick to her stomach.

"You must not blame yourself for this, my dear." Bridget rose and joined Tremble on the rocking loveseat she was sitting in. "He was on a mission. He died valiantly in the line of duty."

"He's still dead and it was because he was working to protect me. I don't like any of this. This is all so very wrong."

"Tremble, make no mistake. The force that killed Anton is ruthless. It will stop at nothing." CeCe turned to face them. Her expression was hard. Her voice was cold.

"You keep calling it a force. What is it or who is it?"

The clouds darkened above. Tremble looked up at the sky and wondered if it was a sign.

"Let's all go inside. It looks like a storm will be here shortly."

Bridget picked up a tray of glasses as Dana retrieved the other items. CeCe closed the umbrella on the table while Tremble pulled the chairs closer to the house. She was the last one through the sliding glass doors. The wind was gaining strength quickly. One of the chairs she had just tried to secure started sliding across the deck. As Tremble latched the door, a bolt of lightning lit up the sky.

"That storm developed quickly."

Dana was already beginning a pot of coffee as Tremble entered the kitchen.

"Unusually quick." CeCe looked out of a window in the kitchen.

The four of them sat around the kitchen table as they waited for the coffee to brew. There was silence until the coffeemaker dinged. Dana rose to get the pot and CeCe began to speak.

"Perhaps some of what I am about to say will make more sense after Laken has recounted the history of our world."

"I must disagree with you, CeCe." Bridget stopped stirring her coffee. "What you are about to tell Tremble is really beyond understanding. You don't understand and neither do I."

"I suppose you are right. We do not understand the darkness that is Scordato."

"The very name gives me chills." Bridget put her hands around the warm mug of coffee.

"We told you about the seven siblings who were the original rulers of the Kingdom of Neverwrong. The number should have been eight. History is rather vague as to the origin of Baldric and Perpetua and the other five sisters. The history of their parents is not even widely talked about. They passed before The Seven came to Neverwrong. Many speculate that is why the sisters, at least, had such a close bond between them. Baldric always seemed like a loner, an outsider in his own family. He was not complete and satisfied." CeCe began the story. "The sisters long referred to a huge library that was filled with countless books. It was a memory they had of their youngest years. They were quite young when they came out of the mountain. Perpetua and Baldric were in their early teens. The first few years of our kingdom were full of chaos and turmoil. Their subjects had been wanderers. They did not wish to be ruled."

"These 'subjects,' as you call them, they were your ancestors?" Tremble interrupted as she tried to piece the account together.

"Yes, that is correct. It is your ancestors, the original rulers of Neverwrong, who bestowed the magical power that we possess upon us. It is an amazing thing. Rare to find rulers who impart some of their own gifts on their people. This is why, for the most part, our allegiance is so strong."

"Very interesting, indeed. Now, go back to talking about Baldric. I think you were about to say something important."

"The sisters spoke of this massive library—a place where all their wisdom was kept. One night, Queen Perpetua dreamed of the location. The following morning, she summoned her siblings. They took a long journey, all by foot, to a mountain high above Tristeza. It was as if the clouds opened up and this beautiful area appeared from nowhere. Several of the servants stood back as The Seven approached an ancient-looking entrance that resembled a cave. It is said that as the siblings reached it, they joined hands and the doorway opened. The Seven walked inside."

"This is my favorite part of the story."

Bridget extended her mug to Dana as she refilled it and CeCe continued.

"This is the part of the heritage that no one likes to talk about. It is where the evil joins the good." CeCe looked deeply into Tremble's eyes.

Tremble saw the pain in CeCe's eyes. It was not an emotion the woman readily showed. It frightened her. As Tremble glanced at her mother, she saw the same look of understanding in Dana's eyes.

"I need to learn this in order to be able to help make this whole mess right, don't I?"

"Indeed you do, my dear girl. I forget how brave you are. It is this resilience that will give you the fortitude to conquer all that lies ahead." CeCe took another drink of coffee.

"We will explain to you later who Meserve is. For our purposes now, I will reveal that he is the one who established the line of Protectors. After what we are about to reveal happened, Meserve decided that the Royals needed to make their most loyal servants a legion of ones who would protect the Royal Family at all costs."

"Like Laken, right?" Dana looked at Bridget and CeCe for confirmation.

"Yes, Laken is a Protector of the highest order. Even though he was created via genetics and magic. He was Anton's son, but not biologically, only genetically."

"That seems like a contradiction?" Dana questioned CeCe.

"It would seem that way in your world. In our world, it is different. It is only in the rarest of circumstances that a being does not come into existence via a true biological process, a male and a female uniting to form an offspring. The creation of Laken was very precise. As mentioned earlier, it is similar to the creation of a child in a laboratory setting. We are told that the egg came from a Royal and the sperm came from a Protector. These two elements were then magically combined to form the embryo that grew to become Laken."

"A Royal? Does that mean that Laken is related to me? This is all so confusing."

Tremble rose from the table. She went to the sink and poured the rest of her coffee down the drain.

"I agree with you. It is very confusing. That's why our goal is to only tell you so much at a time, but it seems that our stories are now becoming jumbled. It is a twisted tale to tell."

CeCe joined Tremble at the doorway that connected the kitchen and the living room. The area was actually one big room separated by a counter.

"The storm appears to be subsiding somewhat. Perhaps, we will be able to go out later to explore the area and find a nice restaurant for dinner."

Bridget entered the living room and sat down as Dana washed up the coffee mugs.

"Laken is a relative of yours, distantly. We do not know exactly, but Belladonna has hinted that the Royal DNA used might have been from one of the other family lines. He is not descended from King Baldric or Queen Perpetua."

"What does Belladonna have to do with this?"

"She was the creator of the spell. It was not felt that Jasmine should be doing such while she was carrying you. This is one of the reasons that he is so close to Belladonna. She has been somewhat of a mother figure to him."

"You also said that he is a descendant of Protector. You said that you were, too." Tremble searched CeCe's face for a clue.

"Anton was my brother."

"Oh, CeCe, we are so sorry." Dana reached out to embrace CeCe, but she only nodded in acknowledgement.

"Yes, thank you." CeCe replied awkwardly and distracted everyone by opening up another screen. "He left us with honor in the service of our Royal family."

Tremble started to say more but stopped as she saw her mother shaking her head.

"Indeed, Anton was a valiant Protector of the highest rank. His knowledge and leadership was a fine basis of learning for Laken." Bridget quickly interceded into the conversation. "CeCe, let's resume telling them about what happened when the Royals went into the mountain."

Tremble and Dana remained silent as the screen changed again. It was closer to the size of the view they had experienced through the picture window in their home. The colors were vibrant and lush and made you want to reach out and touch them. It was like a beautiful oil painting coming to life.

"I've seen this before. I've dreamed this, over and over again."

As Tremble looked deeper at the scene, she realized that it also took on a three dimensional aspect that Laken's imagery had not included. At first, the view was a mountainside. Tremble remembered that the colors in Neverwrong did not match those in the world she grew up in.

"It's incredible to see a red and orange mountain against a green sky."

Dana's eyes were glued to the screen. It reminded Tremble of how her mother always looked in a movie theater.

"It reminds me of autumn, Mom. Except for the green sky, of course."

"Yes, you're right. The most vibrant and beautiful autumn that could be imagined. Oh, look, there went a flock of purple birds."

As Tremble and Dana were entranced by the colors, the view zoomed in closer and closer to the side of the mountain. Tremble began to see an entrance. It looked like a huge rock. As the image focused closer, the rock disappeared. They were immediately inside a dark tunnel-like pathway.

"Wow, these movements can make you feel a little sick." Dana grabbed on to the armrests of her chair. "This is why I don't go to 3-D movies."

"I'm sorry, Dana. We can fix that." Bridget turned to CeCe.

"Oh, no, don't change anything. I will be fine. I love how real everything feels. I'm sure it is important for Tremble to view it this way. Don't worry about me."

Tremble was so fascinated by the images she hadn't realized that CeCe had left the room until she saw her return.

"This will help you." CeCe handed Dana a small vile of liquid.

"What is it?" Dana took the vile and looked at it. The liquid was a lavender color.

"It is a special oil from our world. It has a steadying affect. It is not very potent. Do not be afraid."

"Do I drink it?" Dana took the small cap off of the vile and smelled. "Oh, that is delightful. Smell this, Tremble."

Tremble leaned over from her seat and took a deep sniff. "It's very floral and it sort of tastes like sweet vanilla."

"Tastes?" Dana shook her head. "I keep forgetting that you can do that."

Bridget laughed as she rose to help Dana with the liquid. "Let's just dab a little of this on your wrist. It has soothing powers. You will soon feel very relaxed and your vision will adjust to these additional dimensions."

"Can I try it, too?" Tremble held her wrist out.

"I don't see why not. In fact, let's all have some." Bridget dabbed some on each of their wrists. CeCe shook her head but held her wrist out to join in.

"I'm not going to hallucinate, am I?"

"Oh, Mom, they are not giving us drugs." Tremble paused and looked at both women. "Are you?"

"No, we do not have substances like you refer to as drugs in our world. Beings can have mind-altering experiences though, through magic."

"Bridget, you are getting way off topic. Let's get back to the subject at hand."

Bridget nodded and quickly sat back down in her chair. "Do you feel better, Dana?"

"I feel wonderful. So calm, so steady. What about you, Tremble? Tremble, answer me."

Tremble took a deep breath. "I feel like I have left my body. I can see, hear, feel and taste everything around me, as well as everything on the screen. I also feel like I am floating down the street as I can smell the ocean and feel the sand. What's happening to me?"

"You are discovering what it is like to be from Neverwrong." CeCe smiled. "That is what it is like for Bridget and me every day."

"Hmmm, it's rather cool, but a little frightening."

"Why do you say frightening?" Bridget tilted her head in a questioning manner.

"I don't feel bad or anything. All of the feelings are good ones. It is just strange to be able to see and hear things that are not within your current field of vision or hearing."

"You are making those statements based on the confines of this world." CeCe left her position in front of the screen and walked closer to Tremble. "Think about it this way. You studied astronomy to some degree during your education. In that study, you probably looked through telescopes and were able to see stars that were many light years away. You could see them relatively clearly, correct?"

"Yes."

"Well, then, think of your abilities the same way. Your senses have the ability to distinguish and magnify things that are beyond your immediate area. You can experience your senses beyond the mortal abilities that you are accustomed to."

"It doesn't seem fair. All beings should be able to experience this."

"I agree. Mortals in this world have not taken the time and effort to thoroughly explore and use the senses that they have. Very few take advantage of the capacity that they are born with. But, again, I digress. Onward. Let us enter into the world of your heritage."

The screen changed from the darkness of a long hallway into a vast circular room. It glittered like gold. Soon the screen seemed to engulf the area as if they were in the room from another world.

"Oh my, it's like being in an IMAX theater."

Dana held on tight to the armrests of her chair. Tremble smiled and returned her attention to the vastness of the room. As far as the eye could see, there were shelves and shelves of books, old and beautiful books. It was from them that the golden glow came.

"Wow! That is quite a library." Tremble stood up and looked

around. "There must be thousands of books here." She stopped as she realized they were not alone. "Who are those people behind you?"

"They are your ancestors. King Baldric, Queen Perpetua, and their sisters."

CeCe moved out of the way so that Tremble could see seven people standing near the entrance of the room. They all appeared to be in their teens and early twenties. They were strikingly beautiful.

"They look so regal."

As Tremble's mind began to grasp that the persons weren't really in the room, she walked over and got an up-close look.

"They look like the royalty that they are. These are the most beloved of all the generations of the Royal family. They are the original ones who made all that we know possible." Bridget beamed as she gazed upon them.

"Okay, so what are we doing here? My ancestors are in this massive library. What does that have to do with me?"

"Everything." CeCe and Bridget said in unison.

"What you are about to see was extracted from Perpetua's memory. All of the Royals have given their memories so that future generations could understand what happened. It is the only way that the Protectors were ever able to thoroughly understand what their main purpose was. It tells us who we are up against. Sit down and watch what happens."

CeCe found a spot to stand where she would not block anyone's view of the family. The flickering glow that was coming from the thousands of volumes within her view was very distracting for Tremble. It vaguely reminded her of some long forgotten video game that involved clicking on a dot when it appeared. She forced her eyes to focus on her ancestors. They seemed to be having an argument.

"Why can't we hear what they are saying?"

"Only because you have not allowed your mind to process the words." CeCe gave Tremble a curt nod when she answered her.

"I don't understand."

"Relax your mind, my dear." Bridget sat down next to Dana. "You, too, Dana. Relax your mind. Stop listening with just your ears and allow your brain to hear what your ears cannot."

Tremble closed her eyes. She stopped trying to listen. She just relaxed. At first the sound was faint and she opened one eye to look around. Closing it again, she stopped thinking about listening. She just allowed her mind to wander. A kaleidoscope of colors passed through her vision. It reminded her of the ad agency's logo. She wondered if CeCe and Bridget had gotten the idea for it from a moment of meditation.

As she was lost in that thought, she gradually began to hear voices. First, it was two women, and then a man joined the conversation. Tremble opened her eyes and looked at the group, their lips were moving.

"I do not remember this place at all."

The voice appeared to be coming from the youngest in the group. She was a beautiful girl, barely into her teens, with fiery red hair.

"It was long ago."

The oldest and most beautiful of the young women stroked the girl's hair as she spoke.

"That's my grandmother, isn't it? The oldest one with the raven hair. She's exquisite." Tremble whispered to CeCe who was now sitting beside her.

"Several greats ago, yes. That is Perpetua. You don't have

to whisper. They cannot hear you." CeCe winked and chuckled. "Can you hear them?"

"Yes, I can."

"I can, too," Dana whispered and released her grip from the armrest.

"I knew you were more attuned to your senses than most humans." CeCe gave Dana a thumbs-up. "It has been apparent to most of us who have been Tremble's guardians."

The Seven were walking around throughout the library. Tremble again could hear the conversation.

"It is a beautiful place." The youngest spoke again. "What do you think happened to our parents?"

"Our parents were destroyed by the evil side of nature." Baldric spoke, causing Tremble to tremble. "It is only through the Creator's mercy that we were spared a life eternally within these walls."

No sooner had Baldric spoken than a cold chill ran down Tremble's spine. If it is true that you carry the sins of your ancestors within your genes, then Tremble knew something life changing was about to happen. Tremble looked down as she felt CeCe take hold of her hand. The action diverted her from seeing the person who was coming right up beside her. As she turned, she could see the shadow of something just at her left shoulder. She screamed as the being came into view.

Chapter Eleven

"YOUR SCREAMS COULD raise the dead, my dear."

Bridget jumped off of the coach. Dana did the same and ran toward Tremble. She stopped in her tracks as she saw why Tremble had screamed.

Translucent was the only word that Tremble could conjure to describe him. His skin was so pale and thin that it could almost be seen through. To a bystander, it would have appeared that the two of them were standing face-to-face, inches apart. The truth of the matter was that centuries and a universe separated them.

As she realized her proximity, Tremble began to slowly step backward.

"Darling, he is not in front of you. This is an illusion." CeCe took hold of Tremble's shoulders as she was stepping back. "Do you want me to stop this?"

"No." Her voice was barely audible. "He's so sad looking, yet so beautiful."

"Indeed. You are about to learn why."

They grew silent as they returned to their seats. Tremble could not take her eyes off of the being. He was clothed in rags and was extremely thin. There was not a hair on his head, but his eyes were mesmerizing.

"The eyes, I've never seen someone with deep dark purple eyes." Tremble spoke in hushed tones as those they were watching began to speak.

"Who are you? Identify yourself." Baldric moved to a position between his sisters and the being. All of the sisters, except for Perpetua, stepped back to the doorway.

"Can you not look into my eyes and see who I am?"

The being's voice was melodious. The outer image and the voice did not seem to belong together.

Baldric clutched the sabre at his side. Tremble watched, as he seemed to size up his potential opponent while he slowly moved closer. As Baldric's gaze continued, Tremble saw a look of shock begin to cross his face.

"No. It is impossible."

"Impossible is all my life has been."

Perpetua moved closer to her brother. "Baldric, what are you saying?" Her hand was slowly finding its way to cover her mouth.

"It cannot be. You were gone. We laid you over there." Baldric pointed across the expanse of the room.

Simultaneously, the screen shifted views. They were suddenly seeing the other side of the library. The swift change in perspectives and the three-dimensional view made Tremble's stomach lurch. She heard her mother cry out as they all felt the virtual illusion.

"This is a rough ride, CeCe. Perhaps, we should stop and let Tremble and Dana rest."

"No, we've come this far. I want to know who or what this is."

Tremble looked at her mother. Dana nodded. Tremble took a deep breath and returned her view to the scene in front of them.

Baldric and Perpetua had walked across the room and were looking at what appeared to be an enclosure within a bookcase. A cushion was on top, making it a seat. He glanced at Perpetua before he lifted the cover. As he opened it, the view changed so that Tremble could see inside. It was empty.

"What have you done with—?" Baldric stopped as he saw Perpetua reach out and touch the being's face. There were tears in her eyes.

"Amadeus. Is it you?"

Tremble now realized the being was a man. He recoiled from Perpetua's touch.

"Amadeus is dead. I am Scordato."

"You cannot be." Baldric turned to his sister. "He cannot be Amadeus. Amadeus died. We both saw that he was no longer breathing. We put him in this box and said a prayer over him."

Tremble glanced around the room and saw that the eyes of the sisters were glistening with shock.

"Baldric, look into his eyes. It is our brother. It is Amadeus."

"What? I don't get this. Can you hit a pause button or something?"

Tremble turned to CeCe and Bridget. CeCe waved her hand across the screen and everything disappeared. The room instantly looked lighter. Tremble could hear the ocean waves again.

"You said earlier that the evil force was called Scordato."

"Yes." CeCe began to pace the floor.

"Is that the same Scordato that we just saw?"

"Yes."

"And he is really the brother of Baldric and Perpetua. He is Amadeus."

"Yes."

"Holy crap! This is a mess." Tremble stood up and ran her hands through her hair. There was a sizzle to it, like electricity.

"It certainly is." Dana spoke and everyone looked in her direction. "This is the force that wants to kill Tremble. This person who is one of her ancestors wants to kill my daughter."

"It's not quite that simple." CeCe looked at Bridget. "Maybe we should watch a little more."

"CeCe, do you think that is wise? If Tremble watches much further, she will hear him say, you know."

"I know. Laken will probably not be happy that we are telling the end of the story before he has a chance to tell the beginning."

"Well, actually, this is really the beginning, historically speaking."

"Yes, Bridget, I realize that, but the significance to Tremble's life has its basis in occurrences that happened in more recent decades."

"Will you two please stop bickering and turn the screen back on? I am Tremble, and I have decided that I want to know what this Scordato person has to say."

"Tremble, I am really not sure that it's wise."

"I don't care, Mother. I want to know." Tremble crossed her arms and gave them all a look that said she meant business.

"Very well, as you wish." CeCe made a little bow as with a flick of her wrist the screen again appeared.

"Let us be very clear, Tremble." Bridget had a stern look of her own. "What you are about to hear is your legacy, it is yours and yours alone. As you have already surmised, there is a grave responsibility that comes with your heritage. Your mother, Jasmine, did everything in her power to protect you from it for as long as possible. But, you must face it eventually."

"Bridget's words are very wise, Tremble. I know that your human parents would have given their lives to protect you as your biological parents may still yet do. But, what you are about to hear is your battle. Rest assured though, that you will not be alone to fight it. We dedicated our lives, many of us, knowing full well that the day would come when the prophecy would be fulfilled."

Tremble nodded. She felt ashamed of her forcefulness and lack of patience. All of the people around her had sacrificed so much on her behalf.

"I must learn patience and understanding. I must learn to be appreciative of what has been done for me."

"Understandable. You owe us no apology." CeCe turned back toward the screen, but paused a moment. "Tremble, through the years, I have often wondered how you would react when you learned the truth about your existence. I have wondered if you would rise to the challenge that has been bestowed on you."

"CeCe, you should not be speaking in this way." Bridget's stern look changed to one of disbelief.

"No, Bridget, let her finish." Tremble nodded to CeCe.

"I have wondered how a young woman who had the level of protection that you have experienced would be able to deal with such a discovery. Yet, when you came to work for us a few months ago, I realized something very important. By nature, you come from the union of strength and power unlike our world has ever known. Even more importantly, you were raised by one of the strongest bonds of love that I have ever witnessed in any world. You may not have seen them this way as you grew up, but your Earth parents had the strength, determination, and resilience to raise you, a child from another world, as their own." CeCe gazed in Dana's direction; her eyes glistened. "And, they never faltered for a moment. By nature, by nurture, you are ready for whatever comes your way."

"Thank you, CeCe. I appreciate hearing your confidence in me. You speak the truth. I like the truth. Now, let's watch it. I've got a world to save."

Perhaps it was in that moment that Tremble fully realized it for herself. Like it or not, it was her destiny.

In an instant, the screen came to life. Everything around her paled into the background as Tremble focused her gaze on the man she knew was not only her ancestor, but also her fieriest adversary. She now saw him quite differently. Scordato no longer looked pale and weak. She saw his lean body with muscles rippling throughout. She saw his agile stance like a white panther ready to pounce. His face did not look sunken and thin; she now saw a jaw clinched with determination and anger.

"Yes, Perpetua, I am the one who you called Amadeus. I am the brother that you sang to on the cold nights when we first arrived in this place. I am the boy who went into the garden and came out another person. That weak boy is gone. I am now Scordato."

"Scordato. What kind of a name is that?"

Baldric paced back and forth behind Perpetua. The other sisters were huddled near the doorway. They looked confused and frightened.

"How could Amadeus have survived all these years within the boundaries of this place? It is enchanted. Our own father wove the spell that governs it. I have tried on numerous occasions to re-enter and my power was not able to penetrate it."

"Your power—your power is no match for mine." Scordato snorted. "I broke the original spell years ago. It is my spell that has kept you out. It is my spell that allows you in today."

"I do not believe you. You are nothing but a beggar clothed in rags. You probably crawled through a hole to live in here, in our royal library." Baldric's chest puffed up and he sneered at Scordato.

"I have dressed for your arrival. My appearance is for you, Baldric, for you alone." Scordato turned around and looked in the direction of his sisters. They did not seem as frightened as they were earlier.

Scordato bowed to them and turned around as fast as a child's spinning top. Tremble's eyes could barely take in the speed of what was happening. There were flashes of gold and sparks of color that whirled before them before Scordato again became still.

"Oh my!"

Tremble heard her mother exclaim as her eyes caught up with the image before them. Gone was the pallor of skin and rags that his appearance had moments before included. She noticed that his siblings' reaction was not much different from her own.

He was a different person from head to toe. Jet-black hair lay in soft waves that almost touched his shoulders. His olive skin was a healthy contrast to the translucent white of before. A thick moustache and beard gave a rugged, yet regal, quality to his strong jaw. Broad shoulders filled out a multicolored coat with an intricate design of silk threads. Long pants looked heavy and light at the same time and were in a deep purple, the same color as his mesmerizing eyes.

Perpetua gasped. The other sisters began to walk closer. They were drawn to him. Baldric's expression was smoldering as he saw a likeness that some might say was a mirror of his own.

"Are Amadeus and Baldric twins?"

Tremble allowed her gaze to momentarily leave the screen as she turned to ask her question. She noticed that her mother was clutching a pillow as someone might do when watching a suspenseful movie.

"Yes, they are twins. It makes this story all the worse." CeCe pointed back to the screen.

"I was Amadeus. First born son of Marcellus, the Supreme Enchanter, and her Royal Highness Claudia."

His gaze was like daggers through Baldric. Tremble was amazed to see Baldric break eye contact as if he could no longer stand it.

"You were dead." Perpetua walked toward him. "Baldric was certain that you were dead."

"Baldric was certain. That is true. He was certain that I was alive."

Scordato turned and waved his arm. The floor in the middle of the room opened up and a beautiful jeweled throne appeared from below. Scordato sat down. With another wave a row of seven chairs appeared before him. Each of the sisters made her way to a chair. Tremble could see that there were names engraved in gold on each one. Perpetua stood in front of her chair. Her gaze was on Baldric.

"Tell me that this is not true. Tell me that my beloved brother did not leave his twin in a box to die."

Tremble saw a hardness pass over Perpetua's face. A cold realization that would, no doubt, shape her in the future.

"He cannot do that, my dear Perpetua. He would like to, it is on his lips. Yet, within these walls, he cannot lie to you. My enchantment forbids it."

Scordato cut his eyes toward Baldric and began to laugh. It was a deep, long, and sinister sound, born from his very core.

"Are we here at your bidding? You have waited many years to reunite with your family." Perpetua turned her back on Baldric and sat down facing Scordato.

"It had to be the right time. There were many preparations to be made."

"How have you survived here?"

One of the younger sisters spoke. Her soft voice caused everyone to look in her direction. Her long auburn hair was in ringlets. Alabaster skin framed eyes of emerald green.

"A very good question, Elsavetta." The young woman smiled as Scordato uttered her name. "Look around you. See the vastness of the knowledge on these walls. It is limitless, is it not?" Elsavetta nodded shyly. "My time here has seemed limitless, as well. I have used it wisely."

Scordato rose from his throne and began to walk around the room. Everyone was seated by that point. Everyone, but Baldric. He remained in a corner, like a suit of armor in an old castle.

"Within these walls are the secrets, the secrets to our heritage. These books are filled with the ancient teachings that have long ago dissolved from our ancestors' memories. Knowledge beyond your imagination—the very fabric of everything known from universes, close and far. This has been my nourishment, my family, my world."

Scordato raised his arms and the books seemed to come to life. Sparks of light and energy flickered from them in an array of colors beyond description. It was beautiful and frightening.

Tremble glanced at Bridget. She had never seen the woman look so nervous and unsettled. She and CeCe were always poised and in control. Bridget's behavior now could be described as fidgety and anxious. CeCe was pacing in the back of the room.

Dana caught Tremble's eye and pointed back to the screen. She was no longer clutching the pillow; she was now on the edge of her seat.

"How have you survived in here? Why have you not come to find us?" Perpetua stood and began following Scordato around the room.

"My dear sister, you have failed to understand me. I have learned all of this." Scordato spread his arms out and moved in a circle. "I can do anything. I can create a suit of clothing with a thought in my mind." In a blink, his clothing changed to a vibrant ensemble of emerald green and sapphire blue. "I can summon the forces of the sky." A crack of thunder boomed as lightning lit up the ceiling. The other sisters screamed and cowered. "I can leave this room." Scordato disappeared. "And return before you can see me." They only heard his voice.

"Stop this! You have made a pact with the evil that took our parents. We want no part of it."

Baldric came out from his corner. He looked all around the room. His expression was mixed with anger and fear. Scordato's laughter howled from one corner of the room to the next.

"What a simpleton you are, my brother. I obviously got the looks and the intelligence in our matched birth."

Scordato appeared behind Baldric. He tapped him on the shoulder, causing Baldric to lurch. Scordato continued laughing as he walked away.

"I have visited you on many occasions, my sisters. I have watched as you lovelies have picked flowers in your garden. I have been there as you have walked through the city and visited the commoners in their places of business. I have heard your whispers as you wait in anticipation for the princes from worlds far away to come and ask for your hand."

Scordato returned to his throne and gazed at his sisters. His expression turned to sadness. He bowed his head.

"Tell us. Tell us more." Perpetua smiled as her soft voice beseeched him.

"He calls me evil. The one who left his frail brother here to die calls me evil." Scordato gradually raised his head. His eyes were fixed on something far away. A fire of anger burned within; it made his eyes emit an orange glow. "I have learned truth, these years. I have learned power. Baldric thought he controlled my destiny. I am the one who shall control his and those forever after him. I am the one who shall control all of your destinies."

Scordato rose and looked at each of his siblings individually.

"Unlike my brother, my heart does not wish to cause only harm. Each of you shall prosper. Generations, after you, shall be respected and adored by the common people of this land. Your lives shall be long, but not eternal. You shall be immortal in your consciousness, but not in your physical presence."

Perpetua began to speak, but Scordato held up his hand.

"For you, my dear brother, I have a special prophecy. You shall live to see it fulfilled, but be helpless to render any assistance. Your firstborn shall be a son and each generation shall know a firstborn male. But, when the time comes, when a female is the firstborn heir from your line, she shall destroy your kingdom. The heir shall reject her homeland and desolation shall follow. It is then that I shall regain my birthright and become Supreme Ruler of Neverwrong. I have years of practice in being patient. You must live with the knowledge that your world will someday be destroyed."

"You are making a mockery of our kingdom. Your lies shall not deceive us." Baldric moved to where his sisters were standing. "Sisters, we shall leave this place now. He is a mad man." Baldric pointed for his sisters to go toward the doorway. Slowly, they all obeyed, except for Perpetua.

"Come with us, Amadeus. Put away this folly of evil. Rejoin our family." Perpetua held open her arms and smiled at her brother.

The screen froze as if someone had pushed pause. Tremble turned to find CeCe and Bridget standing behind her.

"Over the next weeks and months and beyond, you will learn many things about Neverwrong and the Royals, The Seven. You will learn deeply complicated spells and historical data that shall make your brain hurt at times. There will be stories that will make you laugh and cry." CeCe paused and turned to Bridget.

"Keeping all of that in mind, what you are about to see is the moment that truly changed your destiny. We want you to pay close attention to what you witness next because we think that within this scene is the secret for you to be able to win out over this prophecy."

Tremble felt an uneasiness begin to grow inside her. Everything she was seeing and hearing was so overwhelming and foreign. Dana drew closer to her daughter and encircled her in an embrace. Tremble sighed in the familiar comfort. It gave her strength. She turned to CeCe and Bridget and nodded.

The scene continued. For an instant, Tremble could see a moment of turmoil cross Scordato's face. He looked longingly at Perpetua. There was love in his eyes. Behind her, Baldric drew closer into Scordato's view. The love left Scordato's eyes and was replaced by an intense anger that almost seemed to seep from his pores.

"No one has asked why I have abandoned my name." He looked from brother to sister. "It is true that Amadeus died. For when you are no longer a part of anyone's life, your very existence slips away. I was nothing but a distant memory to any of you. Even to the one who sealed my fate. Your people do not even know that there was another male offspring. The sacred number of Neverwrong is seven, never eight."

"Amadeus, we did not know. Baldric was but a boy himself."

"A boy who made a man's decision. He cannot look me in the eye and say contrary. Someday you shall know of the humans, the mortals who possess another land. There is a book within these walls that tells their divine story. I have read it many times. In one of its first chapters, brother kills brother. It was familiar to me."

Scordato rose and looked at the walls around him. He rested his hand on his chin and thought for a moment. Then, he raised the same hand. From a wall behind him, a book left the shelf and flew into his waiting hand. It opened and he began to read.

"And his name shall be Scordato, the forgotten one. He shall overcome those who have forsaken him. A child shall be his deliverance from captivity." Scordato closed the book and it flew back to its location on the shelf. "Go forth now, all of you. Leave my midst. I shall bother you no further, for the time. Decades shall pass. You shall not know when this heir shall arrive. She will descend from Baldric, but another of you shall be in her heritage as well."

Baldric motioned for the sisters to go out the door. He moved that way himself. Pausing at the doorway with Perpetua, he turned back.

"You cannot know what was in my heart. You cannot know what I thought was occurring. You have judged me all these years without knowing my true intentions."

"I knew enough. You saw my movement. I was not able to

cry out in my weakened state, but I showed my brother that I had not perished. Your intentions do not matter to me. You never returned." Scordato turned his back on Baldric and Perpetua. "Pray for sons, Baldric. Pray for only sons in your line. A female from your lineage will change everything."

The screen went black. No one said a word for a few minutes.

"I am the female in his line. I am the one he cursed." Tremble rose. Her body hurt all over. Her head felt like it weighed a hundred pounds. "That's why Jasmine hid me, isn't it?"

"Jasmine and Forrest knew their relationship was a risky one. No one from the line of Baldric had married another from the lines of the sisters. It wasn't forbidden as many of the descendants did not have this knowledge. It just was not done. If you had been born a son, it would not have mattered. Jasmine knew that she was carrying a daughter. You would be a female first born in the line of Baldric. Jasmine called up this family memory after she became pregnant. The very next day, she began to make arrangements to come to this world. It is not known if Scordato can travel here, but it is suspected that he has developed his powers to do so."

"Nothing in this indicates that he would do anything to me."

"No, it does not." Bridget began to answer. "But, the prophecy does state that the first heir shall one day be a King. Amadeus is the first heir, even before Baldric."

"How is he even still alive?"

"Remember what Scordato said. 'Your lives shall be long, but not eternal. You shall be immortal in your consciousness, but not in your physical presence.' His brother and six sisters are still alive consciously, even after their physical lives have passed. Remember that you saw Queen Perpetua and King Baldric talk to you from the portraits the other night?"

"Yes."

"They have physically been gone from Neverwrong for many, many years. But, their conscious selves live on that way. That was the curse that Scordato put on them. They know how life plays out for the generations after them. They cannot do anything about it."

"So, is Scordato in some portrait somewhere too?"

"There is much speculation about that. The Royal Army of Neverwrong has long tried to find him."

"It would be nice to be able to see the inside of that library."

Tremble watched as CeCe and Bridget exchanged looks. There seemed to be a conversation going on between the two that neither Tremble nor her mother could hear. As Tremble glanced in her mother's direction, Dana began to speak.

"This certainly has been an intense afternoon. It's way more to grasp than my poor mind can handle. I'm sure that it has been stressful for all of us."

On some level, Tremble could tell that the interaction between CeCe and Bridget had ceased.

"It certainly has been." Tremble took in a deep breath. "I thank you for sharing this with me. I realize that it's probably ahead of the schedule that some had planned on."

"I think that we have had enough of this for now." Dana interrupted before Tremble could ask any further questions. Dana looked around the room and smiled briefly "Why don't we all get ready, and go out and find a nice restaurant for dinner?"

Everyone nodded in agreement. As her mother and CeCe left the room, she noticed that Bridget seemed to be lingering by slowly putting her knitting away.

"Whatever happens, Tremble. Whatever you may later think

about any of us. Remember one thing clearly." Bridget's eyes met Tremble's. "It has never been the intent of a Protector to harm a Royal. Some things are just out of our control."

Bridget turned and left the room before Tremble could reply. She remained there for several minutes in stunned silence.

THE WATER FELT wonderful. Tremble thought she could stay in the shower for the rest of the evening if her stomach didn't think otherwise. She didn't realize how long she had been in the shower until she stepped out from behind the curtain and saw a roomful of steam. She re-entered her bedroom to find her mother stretched out on the bed. Dana had on a cute top and capris, in lime green.

"You look relaxed."

"Looks can be deceiving. You look shriveled." Dana smiled and sat up. "I know your mind must be exhausted. This isn't what you should be doing on summer vacation."

"I think I am getting a little old for that term anyway. Graduation is just beyond the horizon. Of course, I may never reach the horizon."

"Tremble, don't say that; this is just a temporary setback."

"Do you really believe what you are saying or is that straight out of the Mother Handbook?"

"You did not come with a handbook." Dana chuckled and ran her fingers through her hair. "You came with a set of guardians."

"Protectors, I think they call themselves Protectors."

"Indeed. It's a very technical term. They have been consistent and diligent. Your father used to say it reminded him of the Secret Service without the little ear buds. At first, we were aggravated and wanted to be left alone. As the years went by, we realized that they had your best interest at heart, and ours, too. I never would have planned this for you, darling daughter. But, you wouldn't be you without all of this either. I'll leave you to get dressed. Let's just try to take a break from all the darkness we saw earlier and have a fun dinner."

A GENTLE BREEZE crossed Tremble's face as they waited for dinner to arrive. It was a locally owned restaurant that had caught their attention as they explored the small seaside town that evening. Tremble couldn't remember the name, but knew that the word shack was in it. Her mother and CeCe had devoured a dozen oysters on the half shell while she and Bridget had torn into a bucket of peel 'n' eat shrimp. They could hear the ocean waves beyond the small band who serenaded the restaurant's many guests. It was a beautiful coastal night.

"Doesn't this remind you of a winter evening on Edwardia, CeCe?" Bridget motioned to the waiter to bring her another beverage.

"Indeed it does. I remember when Treybo did that special surveillance training there. Were you on assignment then?"

"No, I was still in Earth training. I bet it is rampant with those high profile dead ones during that time of year."

"Overrun with them." CeCe laughed as she ate the last oyster. "It keeps them from making those dangerous trips back to the human world."

"Sightings. Remember the mandate that Belladonna issued about that? She was very adamant. Sightings were becoming too prevalent."

"It always amazed me that so many did not even bother with disguises. It was like they wanted to be caught." CeCe shook her head.

"What in the world are you two talking about? It sounds like the plot of a bad movie."

Tremble handed her mother a basket of hushpuppies. Everyone at the table seemed to be famished.

"Yes, now that you mention it, I believe one of them did make a movie about the experience." Bridget laughed as she peeled another shrimp. "It's not funny when you are sent to fix a slipup."

"Again, what are you talking about?"

"We told you that some of the people that are known as celebrities in the human world are actually from Neverwrong." CeCe's tone became serious. "Well, some of them have gotten tired of life here and exited, suddenly."

"Yes, someone mentioned that before. I thought it was a joke.'

"No, it's not a joke and it can cause problems. Most are happy to return to Neverwrong and live normal lives there. But, occasionally, one will miss something or someone here and will return for a visit. When they are seen, it creates a problem."

"Why is that?" Dana said as she reached for the pail of shrimp.

"Because they were famous here, very recognizable, and they faked their deaths. They are not supposed to show back up again. It starts a mountain of rumors and sometimes, under pressure, they slip and tell about their true heritage."

"And people believe them?" Tremble shook her head.

"No, humans think the person is crazy and they send them

to psychiatric care."

"And it is very hard to get them out of psychiatric care." Bridget smiled as the waiter placed their food in front of them.

"Aren't you concerned that the people around us will wonder what we are talking about?" Tremble gave a forced smile to the waiter. He was about her age and had been very attentive.

"Oh, no, they aren't actually hearing our conversation now. We've put a voice sensor spell up."

"Good grief. Is there anything that a spell can't fix?"

Tremble laughed as she gazed at the unsuspecting people at adjoining tables. They were oblivious to the magic around them. She returned her focus to CeCe and Bridget when she realized that they had become quiet.

"The evil force that wishes to destroy you."

"What?"

"You asked if there was anything that a spell can't fix. I answered; the evil force that wishes to destroy you."

"Scordato. He's an uninvited guest to this dinner."

"He's an uninvited guest everywhere." Bridget took a long drink of her beverage.

"It would appear that is what started this problem." Tremble gave the waiter another fake smile as he served their meal.

Chapter
Twelve

JUST BECAUSE THEY were staying at a beach side house didn't
mean that they would be relaxing. For the next few days,
CeCe and Bridget awakened Tremble early in the morning,
taking her to the beach to teach her how to use her powers. It
amazed Tremble how much of what she found to be normal in
her life wasn't 'normal' for a human at all. She just hadn't recognized the differences.

"I still don't understand how mortals and immortals differ.
Are they genetically the same?"

"We always knew she was a smart one, didn't we? Inquisitive.
Tremble always digs for answers." Bridget smiled at Dana as she
began to answer Tremble's question. "Our genetic structures are
indeed basically the same."

"Tremble, you were born with extra sensitivity. You are pre-
disposed to use it easily." CeCe stood up and began stretching.
"My family and Bridget's, those who have for centuries served

your family, our powers were given to us by The Seven. It was passed to our ancestors in the twinkling of an eye and has been passed from generation to generation since then. We must go through extensive training as children to learn to master it. Some are more successful than others."

"Is it like magic school?" Dana's question made CeCe smirk and Bridget laugh.

"Well, let's just say that it is a little more advanced than primary and secondary education in this realm." Bridget covered her mouth as CeCe scowled at her.

"We do not need to get into this discussion. Tremble will not be attending 'magic school' in Neverwrong." CeCe's tone was curt and her eyes were piercing.

"CeCe does not approve of how Hollywood has depicted witches and wizards being sent off to school and learning all of those grandiose things. My opinion is different. I think it has ever-so-subtly opened up human minds to the possibility that magic can be good and may not be as far removed from them as they think."

"But, really, Bridget, it's all flying broomsticks and crazy potions. It's all fantasy."

"Indeed it is, my friend, but isn't that the point?"

"Touché. Let us get to today's task. Tremble, one of the first things that you must realize is that your brain is programmed for magic. Just as your basic senses work via commands from your brain, your magical sense does as well. It is the seat of your power. I am going to ask you a few questions. First, I want you to answer with the first thing that comes to mind. Then, I want you to think deeply about the question, let your brain study it."

Tremble nodded. She had a feeling that all of these exercises were going to challenge her in ways she never imagined.

"What is the color of a lemon?"

"Yellow."

"Now, think deeper."

Tremble closed her eyes. As her mind relaxed, images began to appear. First, there was a tree with a tiny bloom emerging from the end of a slender dark branch; soon something tiny and green began to burst forth. Slowly, it grew bigger and bigger. It was egg shaped and firm. Gradually, the color changed. The green faded and was replaced by first a light yellow, then a shiny deeper yellow. Tremble thought that the image was complete, but soon her view changed. It journeyed into the fruit. Her perspective delved past the yellow exterior, her tongue could taste the bitter aromatic zest before it felt the soft chewiness of the white pith—a translucent glimmer mixed with the yellow as her senses met the pulp. She wondered if there was such a thing as the color of sour. Suddenly, she encountered a seed; she saw the gray of the seed meet her consciousness. The experience was way beyond yellow. Tremble opened her eyes to find CeCe smiling.

"You've just seen a glimmer of what is to come. All of those sensations are nothing new, but your awareness of them has scarcely begun."

"But, is this magic? Surely there is more to it than that."

"Tremble, if you wish to have the power to conjure a lemon from nothing, you've got to know what is inside its yellow shell. Magic is a most powerful tool to aid you in learning what you need to know. You have to use it wisely. It's reckless to use it without knowing what the results could be. Are you ready?" Tremble nodded. "Mortal or immortal, the universe is broken down into four basic elements. You might think of them as the cornerstones of existence. These are Earth, Water, Fire, and Air."

"I thought that Earth was only the domain of humans."

"I believe that Jasmine partially explained this to your parents, but perhaps we have not been clear to you. Neverwrong and other worlds like it are parallel universes. We occupy Earth as well, only on a different conscious plane. The basics of our ecology mirror that of the Earth that you know. As we talk about the four elements, please remember that they are the foundation of everything. We draw our strength, our very power from these four, and the fifth binds them together."

"The fifth element?"

So mesmerized was Tremble by CeCe's calm and serious words, she did not realize that Bridget had left the beach. She returned in an interesting looking outfit. Tremble almost laughed as she saw the petite woman's garb. Realizing that there was probably some significance to it, Tremble quickly caught her demeanor. The outfit appeared lightweight, easy to move in. The flowing style reminded her of the outfits warn by her father's favorite female singer, Stevie Nicks, during her years in Fleetwood Mac. The top had long sleeves and a fitted bodice, but the sleeves were loose and flowing and came down in long points below Bridget's wrist. The pants were similar in style, fitted at the top before loosely falling to the ground. It was the color that was the most fascinating. It was constantly changing.

Tremble watched as her mother leaned way out of her beach chair to reach Bridget and touch the bottom of her outfit. Tremble gasped as her mother touched the pants leg and the fabric immediately looked like her mother's hand. Dana pulled her hand back quickly as if the action caused her pain.

"Mom, are you okay?"

"Yes." Dana turned to Tremble, laughing. "It just shocked me to see my own hand there." Dana gazed up at Bridget who smiled and began to whirl around.

"This type of outfit is called chameleon, for obvious reasons." CeCe left her spot on the sand and walked over to where Bridget was still twirling. "Let us show you what we mean."

With a flick of her wrist, the scene behind Bridget changed to a busy city street. Bridget's outfit immediately changed and all that could be seen was her head. That was only visible for a split second, and then Bridget was completely invisible.

Tremble rose and walked toward the two women. CeCe was still standing in front of her, but it wasn't until Tremble felt a hand reach out and touch her that she realized that Bridget was still there.

"I can't see you at all."

"I am very much here and you are standing on my foot."

Tremble immediately backed up as CeCe changed the view back to the real location and Bridget began twirling again.

"Don't let the garment deceive you. While it aids in the result, the power to create the chameleon illusion rests within Bridget. It is one of the most useful and difficult spells to cast. That's where we intend to start."

"I don't understand. Why aren't you teaching her something easier and working your way up?"

"That would seem logical and under normal circumstances, beneficial. Yet, we are not going to do that for one specific reason—time. Tremble needs to know how to protect herself. The 'rest' that Belladonna ordered was merely a change in venue. From now on, we must be diligent in training and Tremble must be diligent in learning. Her life depends on it."

When CeCe finished, Dana got up from her chair and began to walk back toward the house.

"Where are you going, Mom? I'm okay with this. I know I have to get serious."

"I realize you do. You have always been a serious child. I think I have done all that I can do to help you up until this point. Now, these ladies and others like them will have to do the rest. I'm going to go do the one thing I know that I can to help."

"What's that, Dana?" The look on CeCe's face showed concern.

"I'm going to cook. I would say that all of this training is going to make all of you hungry. Perhaps, you will teach Tremble eventually how to whip something up the Neverwrong way." Dana moved her hands in the air as if casting a spell. "Until then, I will do it the old-fashioned way. Ladies, Tremble has a lot of favorites, I hope you will enjoy them. CeCe, where are the car keys?"

"I'll get them for you." Bridget started to follow Dana. "I must also give you Belladonna's credit card. All of this goes on our expense account."

"Belladonna has a credit card?"

Dana continued to ask questions as the two women briskly walked through the sand back to the house. As Tremble turned back toward CeCe, she saw that CeCe was smiling.

"There have been a couple of other cases in our history where someone from Neverwrong has tried to hide a child in this world. None of them ever worked. Protectors had to come in and do some serious memory sweeps. Part of our training includes viewing things that went wrong and learning from them. Two exceptional humans raised you. Please do not ever forget that."

"Oh, I know my folks were phenomenal parents. I had a great childhood."

"You are missing my point. Before you were even born, they agreed to become human shields against an unimaginable non-human force. As I understand, Jasmine was quite frank with them in the final days of her pregnancy. She gave them one last chance to back out. She told them that while the framework had been laid to conceal you until adulthood, in all likelihood that would be penetrated. The very first thing that would have happened was that your parents would have been killed as well as anyone who might have gotten in the way. Jasmine had the power to read their feelings and intentions. Neither one of them flinched. All she felt was love; love for you. Love for a child they had not met. Just imagine that, Tremble. They had no biological connection to you. They hardly had the slightest of relationships with your mother. But, their love, separate and combined, has been every bit as strong as the spell that Jasmine put on you. Belladonna is convinced that love has been your truest protection. Don't ever forget. It will serve you well one day."

Tremble let her gaze drift to the ocean as she thought about what CeCe had just told her. She had never doubted her parents' devotion. Even during her early teens, when rebellion seemed fitting, she always felt like they were on her side. In her wildest imagination, she never would have guessed the secret they had so carefully hidden or what that secret must have cost them along the way.

"CeCe, the fifth element, the one that you say binds all the others together. You didn't finish telling me what it was."

"It is the Spirit. It is what binds everything we do and everything we are. You must learn to respect it, to honor it, and to use it."

Tremble thought about CeCe words and everything that she had learned so far on this incredible journey.

"I'm ready, CeCe. There are a lot of people that I don't need to let down. Teach me how to overcome Scordato."

FOR THE NEXT couple of hours, CeCe and Bridget took turns lecturing about the fundamentals of magic and showing Tremble how the illusion spell worked.

"Tremble, you are not concentrating. You need to be able to reach a meditative state quickly and stay there. Otherwise, this is going to keep happening."

The 'this' that Bridget was referring to was the state that Tremble was currently in. A view had been placed around her that mimicked the look of a forest. After several attempts of concentration and spell chanting, Tremble had begun to get a handle on becoming a chameleon. The only problem was it only seemed to work on certain parts of her body. Both legs and her left arm were now invisible, but she couldn't seem to get her right arm and head to 'chamel' as Bridget referred to it.

"This look will have the opposite intended effect. You look like you are reaching out from the middle of that tree. Let us try this one more time before we break for lunch. Come completely back and we will start again."

It amused Tremble that the way you let go of a chameleon effect was to shake yourself like a dog shaking off water. After Tremble had completely 'returned,' she stood facing Bridget and mimicked the woman's words and actions.

"Do you always start with your arms by your side and your hands made into fists? That seems tense."

"It is a pose that does not draw attention if you are forced to go into this mode in a crowd."

CeCe had been doing her own meditating on a beach towel in the sand. She joined them as Tremble was shaking off her last attempt.

"As I have told you, you must relax your mind. Clear your thought patterns. Focus on translucent. Dimming light. Weightlessness. Repeat after me." Bridget opened one eye to see if Tremble's eyes were closed. Tremble quickly closed them. "Wind and feathers. Light and air. Whirls of color. Thoughts forebear. All illusion, nothing seen. Tremble shimmers in her dreams."

"It doesn't make much sense."

Tremble had opened her eyes midway through Bridget's chant. Bridget took a deep cleansing breath before she opened her eyes.

"It doesn't have to make sense. The chanting is not what makes the spell work. It is merely a tool to get your mind where it needs to be. All magic comes from within your mind. That's why the most skilled enchanters can work a spell without ever uttering a word."

"I want to be a skilled enchanter."

Tremble hadn't realized she felt that way until the words had left her mouth. She closed her eyes and relaxed her mind. As she began to see soft circles of light, she realized that she had reached the point she needed to be. She began to speak.

"Wind and feathers. Light and air. Whirls of color. Thoughts forebear. All illusion, nothing seen. Tremble shimmers in her dreams."

Slowly, she opened her eyes and looked down at herself. All she saw was the forest.

"Bravo, my dear. Bravo. Queen Perpetua would be proud."

Chapter Thirteen

"**I** KNOW THAT YOU do not remember doing this, but this is one magic skill we both feel you will ace in no time. Again, it is a very important way to get you out of situations that are about to become troublesome or dangerous."

Bridget and CeCe had decided that Tremble's afternoon of training would be held indoors. Both of them said they were tired from the morning's activities, but Tremble knew they were really just painfully full. Dana had taken her task very seriously. She had gone to a local fishing pier and bought an assortment of fish and seafood fresh out of the ocean. A stop at the farmer's market had completed their menu. Not only was a lovely seafood salad waiting for them when they broke for lunch, but also some seafood bisque, a green salad full of crunchy veggies, and some delightful homemade bread. Tremble was glad that she had conquered the chameleon spell before the meal. There was now more of her to make disappear.

"As Bridget was saying, this one you have done before, only not intentionally."

"I know what this is going to be."

Dana shouted from the kitchen. Tremble was sure she smelled the beginnings of her mother's lasagna. They were all doomed for stretch pants.

"Yes, indeed you do, Dana."

Tremble was happy to hear Bridget's laugh. Everything had seemed so serious.

"Okay, is this when I pulled the Minnie Mouse thing you all were talking about the other day?"

"Exactly. I realize that your father made you promise that you wouldn't do that again, so it was not a developed skill."

"Well, here's the thing. There have been a few times that I have accidentally broken that promise."

Dana's mother-radar must have managed to pick up from two rooms away.

"What?"

All eyes turned in her direction. She was leaning over the counter bar area that separated the kitchen from the dining area.

"You all have to understand, I don't remember the Minnie Mouse incident and sometimes my temper can get the best of me." No one said a word; they all just stared at her, waiting. "There was this time in high school. I hadn't studied for the geometry test. I was standing at my locker getting my books and I said to myself, 'I wish I was home.' In a blink, I was home. It scared me so bad that I thought I was sick. I took a couple of aspirin and put myself to bed." Tremble looked at her mother. "Dad was asleep from a long night in surgery. When he got up later, I asked him to check me out. I never told anyone what happened."

"Were there any other times?" CeCe's tone was more curious than stern.

"One other time."

Dana came into the room, drying her hands on a towel. She looked concerned.

"It was my freshman year in college. I was having a rough time with one of my suitemates." Tremble turned to Dana. "Remember Mazey?" Dana nodded. "She was a little crazy."

"Crazy Mazey?" Bridget covered her mouth as a giggle escaped.

"I remember that she moved out rather suddenly."

"Yes, I wished her away."

"Wait a minute. I thought you were about to tell us about you willing yourself to another location. You mean you did this to another person?" CeCe's tone had turned back to serious.

"Yes, I guess so. She never came into our dorm room again, as far as I know. She ended up in a dorm on the other side of campus. Everyone acted as if we knew this was going to happen. I decided to go along with the act. I actually was trying to convince myself that I wasn't crazy."

Dana came up from behind Tremble and encircled her in an embrace. "You are anything but crazy. I am so sorry you went through this by yourself."

"It's okay. I was still a teenager then. You know, teenagers can adapt. I chalked it up to being part of my college adventure." Tremble paused, lost in thought. "I have seen Mazey a couple of times since. She doesn't act like she even knows me."

CeCe and Bridget exchanged looks.

"Something sure is smelling wonderful, Dana."

Bridget's attempt to change the subject did not go unnoticed.

"What are you two thinking? It wasn't me who made Mazey

move?"

"It's part of the learning process, CeCe. I don't think that now is the time to start hiding things from her."

"Tremble, willing yourself somewhere is one thing. It's all about you, your power, your movement. Willing someone else is a whole other ballgame. It's not that you do not have the power to do that. You don't have the skills. Just a pure wanting, wishing, on your part would not make it happen. You had help."

"Help? Who?"

Tremble saw a look cross CeCe's face that she had never seen from the woman before. She saw fear.

"I have no idea."

"I HAVE BEEN reading these books for hours. Aren't there *Cliff Notes* versions? These paragraphs go on and on."

After the earlier revelation, CeCe and Bridget left Tremble with a stack of books to read. They said they were going on a drive, but Tremble suspected they were getting in touch with Belladonna to try and figure out who may have helped Tremble get rid of her suitemate. While the lasagna was baking in the oven, Dana had gone for a walk on the beach. Tremble was alone with the books for an hour.

"We thought you would enjoy experiencing those books. They aren't like any you would check out from a mortal library."

"I admit they are very interesting. But, good grief, do they have to be so technical?"

"We never said that magic would be easy."

"What makes the books so unusual?"

Dana joined them on the deck as she placed a steaming dish

of lasagna in the middle of the table. Bridget followed from behind with a bowl of salad and a basket of bread.

"Take a look at one, Mom."

Tremble watched as her mother opened one of the books
from the pile that was beside her. She flipped through a few pages, and then looked back at Tremble.

"It just seems like a regular book. What am I missing?"

"You don't see anything unusual?" Tremble furrowed her
brow as she looked from the book to her mother.

"No, Tremble. Dana cannot see what you see." Bridget came
up behind Dana and patted her on the shoulder. "But, we can
show her."

"Tremble, up until this point we have allowed your mother to
see and experience many of the things that you are experiencing
for the first time. We thought it would be beneficial to her to be
involved so that she can continue to be supportive of you and
have an understanding." CeCe sat down at the table. "But, Dana
is a mortal, and doesn't naturally have the abilities that you do.
If all mortals could experience what we do, well, they wouldn't
be mortals."

"Dana's mind is open to all things magical. We have seen
many times, through the years, that she can pick up on glimmers
of the magical world. It was probably a subliminal factor that
drew Jasmine to her."

"Excellent point, Bridget. Belladonna has quietly speculated,
Dana, that you may have a little magic in your background."

"Well, I don't know about that." Dana laughed as she began
serving the lasagna. She stopped as CeCe handed her a plate.
"Actually, my grandmother used to tell a story about her grandfather. She always said that he came from a faraway land and could
make things happen."

"It is very possible that he might have been magical. If not from Neverwrong, perhaps from another kingdom. The possibilities are endless."

"Endless?" Tremble stopped with salad tongs in her hand. A clump of green salad was dangerously near collapse over the breadbasket.

"Perhaps 'endless' is not the best word." Bridget moved the breadbasket from underneath the floating salad. "There are many other magical kingdoms besides Neverwrong."

"I wonder if their heirs are being chased by an evil force." Tremble smiled at her mother as she placed a healthy portion of lasagna on her plate. "Oh, Mom, I dream about this. It is so delicious."

"Why don't you let your taste buds be the judge of that first and not your Neverwrong senses?"

"Ah, you are developing a magical sense of humor, Dana. It is delightful."

Italian cheeses were dangling from Bridget's fork as she started to take a bite.

"Oh, but my Neverwrong senses are never wrong, are they?"

"Everyone is a comedian." CeCe slung her long black hair over her shoulder.

Tremble decided it was time to ask two of the many questions that were on her mind.

"I've got a question. Actually, I have many."

"Ask away. Knowledge is power." The lasagna seemed to have somewhat calmed CeCe.

"Neverwrong. Where did the name come from?"

"An excellent question, indeed." Bridget smiled as she reached for another slice of bread. "It is a wonderful story. You shall have the opportunity to read the Letters of Perpetua. Our first queen wrote extensively about the years that The Seven had with their parents before they came out of the mountain. As we understand, it was Perpetua who gave our kingdom its name. Her letters tell us that their father, Supreme Enchanter Marcellus, had an adage that he frequently told his children—you are never wrong when you do what is right. It was her idea to bestow magical powers onto the commoners of the land, my and CeCe's ancestors. She thought it was the right thing to do. So, our land was called Neverwrong."

"That is lovely." Dana had stopped eating and smiled, turning to Tremble. "That makes me feel very good about your ancestors. At least most of them seem to have had good principles."

Everyone resumed eating. Tremble kept thinking about this far away land that she had many connections to and none at the same time. Her thoughts drifted to the main person who was charged with her wellbeing now.

"Can we talk about Laken? I have a lot of questions about him."

"Certainly, Tremble. That is understandable. He is going to become a larger part of your life."

"Well, that's a good place to start. I don't exactly understand. What is his purpose?"

"Allow me, CeCe, I know that parts of this will be difficult for you." Bridget turned to Tremble and began to speak.

"Oh, I'm sorry, CeCe. I forgot that Laken's father was your brother. All of these layers of people and relationships are confusing."

"Do not fret, Tremble. I am fine with speaking of Anton. As I said before, he died with honor serving our Royal family. I am proud of Laken and the work he has and will do with you. I will let Bridget tell you the bulk of the story while I go take a shower." CeCe patted Bridget on the shoulder as she left the room.

Tremble watched as her mother resumed her task of taking the dishes away as she and Bridget followed her with the leftover food. They were silent for a while, content to let the clatter of dishes be the conversation.

"Tremble wants to know more about Laken. Let that dishwasher work its magic and we can go watch the sun set from the deck."

Dana pushed the 'on' button as Bridget led them out of the room. The sky was red with layers of yellow and gold. It might have been one of the most beautiful sunsets that Tremble remembered seeing.

"What do sunsets look like on Neverwrong?" Dana was the first to speak as the three relaxed on the deck.

"They are equally as beautiful as yours are here, only our colors manifest themselves in a different manner. First of all, our sun is blue, a rich sapphire. It gives off a more calming effect than your sun. No one needs to wear sunglasses in Neverwrong. Our sky is yellow and it constantly glistens. As the sun sets, the combination of blue sun and yellow sky produces—"

"Green. Yellow and blue makes green."

"Yes, Tremble. The same principle applies in Neverwrong. In fact, it is where that phrase was coined. So, to answer your question, Dana, our sunsets are all of the beautiful shades of green you can imagine and some that go beyond imagination. It is soothing, restful, and inspiring. It may be what I miss the most from our world."

Tremble watched Bridget in silhouette. It was obvious the woman was lost in thought. Knowing a little about her powers, Tremble wondered if she was, at that very moment, travelling to Neverwrong for a brief visit to see one of those green sunsets. It was hard for Tremble to imagine, to wrap her mind around, the concept of a whole other world, and that she herself belonged in it.

She returned her gaze to the setting sun. As she stared into it, an incredible thing began to happen. Her view began to change. Slowly, as if by the strokes of a paintbrush, the rich reds and golds of her own sunset disappeared and were replaced by blues and yellows, and then finally green. The colors reminded her of the rich colors she had seen in the colorization of old movies. It beckoned her.

Tremble could hear someone speaking, but her trancelike state could not be broken. She was becoming one with her view. Through the sunset, she could see someone walking toward her. The person wore a long black robe with a hood. The rich green rays coming off of the sunset concealed the face, but the person's hands were reaching out to her. They were the hands of a woman.

"Tremble!" As she opened her eyes, it was the hands of her mother that she saw shaking her. "Where did you go?"

"I don't know. It was beautiful." Tremble stopped herself from telling what she had seen. She turned to Bridget. "I think you need to tell me all I need to know about Laken. I need to know as much about everything as soon as I can."

Bridget's eyes darted back and forth as she seemed to process what Tremble was saying. A look of concern, followed by resolution replaced her normal bubbly expression. With Dana still huddled next to Tremble, protecting her in a strong embrace, Bridget began her story.

"It came to Jasmine in a dream, we are told—a dream she walked through and lived; a dream that would come true through her own hand. The vision visited her sleep in the early weeks of her pregnancy. It is said that before it was revealed that your birth was pending, she would awaken for many nights with this vision. As she told Forrest, your father, about it, he was convinced that it was a divine instruction that should be closely followed."

"How is it that you know so much about this, Bridget? This is not information that Jasmine relayed to us." Dana loosened her grip on Tremble before she asked her question.

"Those of us who have served as Tremble's guardians were given very specific and thorough training. The information I am telling you is the background to the creation of Laken. In the early years of our work, some were not as thorough regarding their assignments as they should have been. I am sad to say that there were holes in Tremble's protection. Thankfully, each time one of our officers faltered, there was another skilled and dedicated officer to fix the problem. Belladonna made sure that future Protectors' training was enhanced. She became very transparent with her knowledge in this regard to make it so."

"Belladonna sounds very wise. It is a trait that she shares with her sister."

"Your words are true, Dana. She has devoted her life to Tremble's and Jasmine's safety and well-being." Bridget cleared her throat and took a drink of iced tea. "The idea of creating a Protector exclusively for Tremble came to Jasmine in this dream. She said that she saw a vision of her child, her daughter, as a young woman and that there was a young man who was constantly with her. His stature indicated that he was in a protective role, but to her it was not one that had come via family, such as a brother, or via love, such as a suitor. It appeared as what this world considers a bodyguard—someone who would stand between a person and harm. The Royal Family has always had Protectors of some sort."

"So, what makes Laken so special?"

"Laken was created specifically for this role. His existence was patterned after Jasmine's dream."

"That sounds a little weird."

"I can see how it would to you. But, remember, your birth was part of a prophecy. Your existence affects the entire future of Neverwrong. In other words, the whole story of you is a little weird."

"And somehow that is the part that I don't mind so much." Tremble laughed causing the other two to join her.

"Jasmine felt that she could not be the one to create Laken. So she gave this task to Belladonna. CeCe's family had been Protectors from the beginning. Anton was very dear to Jasmine's parents, so much so that at one point it was speculated that he might be allowed to marry Belladonna."

"Were they in love?"

Tremble noticed that Dana had her 'watching a movie' face on again. She could become totally enthralled in a story.

"I am not sure that I have the knowledge to properly answer that question. But, I do know that they were close from childhood. Anton was also close to your parents. They were all friends. Belladonna studied the idea of the creation of a special Protector for her niece. She knew this being would need to have the correct mixture of Protector genetics and Royal genetics in order to not only be able to guard you, but also understand you. Anton was her obvious choice, and he readily agreed to be involved. We do not know where the Royal side of the genetics combination came from."

"You don't think that it came from Belladonna herself?"

"No, we know that for a certainty. She told us that she did not have the strength that Jasmine did. She could not give her child to another for the greater good. We imagine that it came from one of the sister families."

Tremble stood up, stretched, and rubbed her fingers on her temples. Her head was throbbing, not so much with pain, but with information overload. She wished that she had time to get in a run. All of these stories made her mind and body tense.

"I think it is fine for us to take a break now. A moonlight run would probably do you good."

"Do you have the ability to read my mind constantly?"

"No, I am not a mind reader at all. Your actions spoke louder than words." Bridget laughed. "You go for a run. I will take a shower and change into my jammies while you are gone. Perhaps do a little reading. I will give you the rest of the basics of Laken's story before we go to bed."

After quickly changing, Tremble was off down the beach. The ocean breeze was intoxicating. The sound of the waves relaxed her on a level she could not put into words. She wondered how much longer the freedom to do something as simple as run would be hers. They had already been at the beach for a couple of days. She wished she could say that she understood her situation better. The fact was that she didn't. She wondered if she ever would.

The beach was empty so Tremble pushed herself. She set a goal to run as far as the pier, a good two miles, by her estimate, before she turned back. She felt a little tension starting to return to her body the closer she got to the beach house. It was as if she could detect that something was about to change. She saw the change sitting on the steps that led to the house. Laken was waiting for her.

"What are you doing here?"

"Hello, Tremble, nice to see you, too." Laken rose from the

steps.

"I'm sorry. I just wasn't expecting to see you. Good evening, Laken. To what do I owe this pleasure?" Tremble gave him a little bow.

"I should not have said that. Please forgive me. I seem to have lost all my sense of humility and decorum. Forgive me, Princess Tremble."

"Oh, no. That stops right now. I will not be called Princess. Nope. Not going to happen." Tremble held up her hand as Laken started to reply. "Did we know you were coming?" Tremble's mind went to the conclusion of the conversation.

"No. My meeting with Belladonna ended suddenly so I thought I would come and be of assistance with your training."

"I thought I was supposed to be relaxing." Tremble wanted to see how much of her minute-to-minute activities her personal Protector knew.

"That may have been Her Royal Highness' initial directive. But, I am sure that CeCe and Bridget have used this time to give you instruction."

There was a light on a pole at the bottom of the steps. It was what had allowed Tremble to initially see that someone was sitting there. This artificial glow would in most cases not make a person appear to look healthy. Somehow it seemed to have the opposite effect on Laken. He looked older. He looked more handsome with his square jaw and high cheekbones. His eyes sparkled, but he had a look of tiredness and anguish at the same time. He looked troubled.

"Are you okay?" Tremble asked as they began to climb the steps.

"Rest has not been my companion."

"I suppose I am your companion now, huh?"

"That would be correct. From now on, you are stuck with me."

"Till death do us part," Tremble laughed, but quickly added. "I am just joking."

"I certainly hope not."

As they climbed the stairs in silence, Tremble wondered if it really mattered to her to which part of her reply Laken had responded.

"Look who I found on the beach."

Dana, CeCe, and Bridget were lounging in the living room watching television. Meryl Streep was pretending to be a French chef.

"Bon Appetit!" The three women said it in unison followed by hearty laughing.

"I said, look who I found on the beach."

"We know Laken is here. We told him where you were."

CeCe's eyes did not leave the television screen, but Bridget looked at Tremble. It was an understanding look. Their conversation was not over.

"My journey here has been complicated. I am very tired. I think I will go to bed."

Laken pulled off his jacket. He was wearing a T-shirt. Tremble had not seen him in short sleeves before. His body-builder arms visibly shocked her.

"I apologize for my casual attire. I thought it would be more appropriate since I was coming to the beach."

"Laken, we weren't planning on you being here." CeCe rose from her chair.

"He can have my room." Dana rose and headed down the hallway. "I believe there are two queen beds in your room, isn't there, Bridget?"

"Absolutely, why didn't I think of that? It will be like being in college again. We can sit up all night and giggle."

CeCe shook her head. "Dana, you do not have to give up your room. I can share Bridget's room."

"No, CeCe. I think Dana is right. You snore."

"Dana may snore, too."

"At least it would be a new snore. I've heard your snoring from time to time for decades."

Tremble laughed. As serious as the two women could be, they seemed to argue over the silliest things.

"I am fine to sleep on a couch."

"No." All three of them were in unison again.

"You all sort it out. I'm going to hit the shower and say goodnight. I presume that I have another early morning ahead of me." Tremble began climbing the stairs to the loft.

"I have a briefing from Her Royal Highness to go over with CeCe and Bridget."

"I'm not privy to the briefing?" Tremble stopped on the stairs and looked back at Laken.

"Actually, no."

"What about me?" Dana had re-entered the room with the sheets from her bed in her arms.

"You can come."

"I'm supposed to be the heir to a magic kingdom and I have no privileges at all?"

"It is imperative that those in your legion of guardians understand Belladonna's directives first so that they may assist in carrying them out."

"Oh, Laken, you would be so much more fun if you weren't such a stuffed-shirt." Tremble resumed walking up the stairs.

"I do not understand this phrase. Is my shirt too tight?"

This time, all four women howled with laughter.

Chapter Fourteen

TREMBLE SAT STRAIGHT up in bed. She was shaking all over. Her heart was pounding. As she swung her legs over the edge of the bed, she tried to make her jumbled mind sort out what she had experienced during her dreams. The location was blurry and unfamiliar, but the person she saw was close to her heart. Only it wasn't him really, was it?

"You did not sleep well."

She almost jumped out of her skin as she realized that Laken was quietly sitting in her doorway. She rubbed her eyes as she saw he was in Superman lounge pants and a soft looking Henley shirt. It looked like a bad Christmas present. He was trying to fit into her world.

"What are you doing here? How long have you been sitting there?"

"I hope my presence does not distress you. Your restless dreams awakened me about an hour ago. I hoped that my close presence might calm you."

"You can see my dreams?"

"No, not at all. I can sense your emotional reactions to them. This dream troubled you, confused you. Am I correct?"

"Yes, most definitely. Why? How can you do this?"

"I was created to be your Protector. In a combination of genetics and magic, I am designed to tune into you. In human terms, I have Tremble radar."

Laken laughed and Tremble saw what she might have called his human side. In normal circumstances, she probably would have sought this guy out as a friend, or maybe more. Sitting in the floor of her bedroom, he seemed like a dozen nice guys she had met in college. Those guys couldn't feel her dreams though. Their existence hadn't been predetermined before her birth. She couldn't imagine how this relationship would ever be anything but awkward.

"Do you want to tell me about your dream?"

She thought carefully about his question before she answered it. How much should she tell him about her thoughts and feelings? Would it help or be a hindrance as this journey continued?

"I don't know where I was in the dream. It was not a familiar location to me. The person in the dream was very familiar by sight."

"By sight? What do you mean?"

Tremble stood up and walked toward the window. The sun was starting to rise and a little morning light filtered in through the curtains. She looked down at herself, realizing she was dressed in her nightclothes. Somehow, she wasn't the least bit uncomfortable being that way in front of Laken. Was it that college dorm feeling? She had lived in a coed dorm for her first two years and got used to seeing those on her floor, male and female, in just about everything and sometimes nothing. Or was it some sort of spell that had been cast to make her accept him as her Protector?

"The person in the dream, physically, was my father. But, it wasn't his voice. It was a voice I have never heard, yet it was familiar somehow."

"Tremble, this could be very important. I think it might be a good time for me to teach you about something that you can magically do to allow me to hear that voice."

Tremble tilted her head and gave Laken a questioning look. "I don't understand."

"Allow me to demonstrate." Laken stood up and put his index and middle fingers on each of his temples. With his eyes closed, he looked to be deeply concentrating. "Dream stored deep in mind come out from where you hide."

Laken moved his fingers from both sides of his head and made a straight line in front of him. Instantly, Tremble could see an image on a screen like the others that Laken and CeCe had shown her. In this image, Laken appeared to be in the air flying. He was playing some sort of a game. Tremble laughed as she realized that he was balancing himself on something similar to a surfboard. She watched as Laken threw what appeared to be a triangular shaped ball toward a square opening that she presumed was a goal of some sort.

Tremble turned and watched Laken view the image. He had a big smile on his face like it was a real memory. "I didn't realize you were an athlete in Neverwrong." As she looked back at the screen, she realized that she had already begun to recognize the landscape of the land of her heritage.

"I'm not an athlete, at least not in the sense that you see before you. I've never played a team sport." Tremble gave him a confused look and pointed to the screen. "I've just dreamed of playing. This is one of my dreams. I'm going to show you how to do this."

"Right, sure. That's hilarious, Laken."

"Just humor me. Follow my directions. What do you have to lose?"

Tremble shook her head. "Okay."

"Put your fingers on your temples as I did. Close your eyes and think about the dream you had last night. Have it firmly planted in your conscious thought, and then repeat this phrase."

Laken stopped and waited for Tremble to do what he had said. After she had put her body in the correct position and closed her eyes, he continued.

"Think about it. Remember it. Now, repeat this. 'Dream stored deep in mind come out from where you hide.'"

With her eyes shut tight, she began to remember the dream that had awakened her. She saw a blurry image, and then her father came in clear view. It made her smile to see his face. When he opened his mouth and began to speak, her smile immediately vanished. She began to repeat. "Dream stored deep in mind come out from where you hide." As she opened her eyes, she moved both of her hands from her head straight in front of her as Laken had done. For an instant, she saw a flicker of the image before her. With a shocked smile, she looked at Laken.

"That's good, very good. Outstanding, for a first time." He beamed at her, giving a thumbs up. "Try again. Deepen your concentration."

Closing her eyes again, she did as he said. She blocked out everything else in her thought pattern and began to relive the dream in her mind. She soon realized that she had been so shocked to see her father's face with another voice that she really hadn't paid attention to what the voice was telling her. She began to chant. "Dream stored deep in mind come out from where you hide."

Tremble made the motion with her hands in front of her without opening her eyes so as not to disturb her concentration. Before she could open them, she heard Laken shout.

"Excellent! On the second try. Your powers are vast and amazing. Belladonna will be so impressed."

There before her on a screen in full vibrant color was her dream. The background was dark green in color. It reminded Tremble of a forest. Her father's beautiful face shone in the forefront. There were no signs of the cancer that had left his body as a shell of his former self. This was the healthy vibrant man who put thousands of people back together, yet could not operate his own elaborate VCR. She motioned for Laken to listen as he began to speak.

"Tremble, my dear, please forgive me for using the image of the one you loved so deeply. I knew that you would not recognize me or even possibly remember a dream with a stranger within it. I mean no disrespect to the man who did what I could not."

Tremble gasped and turned to Laken. He came toward her, shaking his head. He encircled her in an embrace. It momentarily felt awkward, but the feeling vanished quickly as the voice continued.

"My deepest wish is that Jasmine and I could have raised you ourselves. Our love was selfish. Our hearts could not be apart. Our destinies could not deny that we would have a daughter unlike any other in the history of our world. It saddens me that you were born with a prophecy over your head. Jasmine and I should have prevented it, but, alas, we desired to have our own child. We loved you before we created you."

Laken left Tremble's side and retrieved a chair from a small desk nearby. Tremble slowly sat down, never taking her eyes off of the image of her father. As Laken knelt beside her, the voice of Forrest continued.

"I come to you now in your sleep because you are finally aware of your heritage. The knowledge that you have spent all of these years not knowing about the existence of your mother and me has almost been as devastating as being separated from you. I was not there for your birth. I did not have the opportunity to hold you in my arms as this man who I now speak through did on a regular basis. For many long years, I stayed as far away as I could; only daring to touch your forehead for a moment, once, as you slumbered in your dreams."

As the man she assumed was Forrest said these last words, tears began to fall down Tremble's face. It was unimaginable for her to fathom that this man whose voice she had never before heard, for a moment, shared the same air with her.

"I must hurry before you awaken. I have come to you now with a warning, strong and bold. The spell that your mother so carefully wove around you is now dwindling. By the twenty-first anniversary of your birth, the protection shall be gone. I trust that you will have many of our finest guardians surrounding you, teaching you about your own powers."

Laken squeezed her hand as she looked in his direction. When she started to speak, he motioned for her to be silent and pointed back to the screen.

"Listen, my child, pay careful attention. While the world you were raised in has little or no knowledge of the Kingdom of Neverwrong, our realm is known and respected by all in the immortal world. Your mother and I have had the assistance of other kingdoms of magic far and wide. I trust that by now, you have been given at least a rudimentary lesson regarding the evil force that dares to challenge your existence. I hope that you also know that what makes him far worse than any other enemy is that he shares your blood. How horrid it is for your own family to wish such devastation on your kingdom and its heir. But, I must admit that Scordato, as he wishes to be known, did have an unforgivable sin invoked upon him by his own brother. Yes, his twin. I do not deny it."

By instinct, Tremble raised her hands, palms out, and swept them in front of the screen. The voice stopped, as if it has been paused.

"How did you know to do that?" Laken's eyes grew big as he saw what Tremble had done.

"I don't know. It just came to me to do it. I had to stop it a moment so that I could process what I have heard. How can it be that this voice that possesses my father's body is Forrest, the being that is biologically responsible for my birth? I don't understand."

"For King Forrest to come out of hiding to speak to you, even in your dreams, his message must be of extreme importance. When I sensed the troubling restlessness of your dreams last night, I knew that something crucial was being conveyed to you. This message coming from your father is beyond the bounds of my imagination. You must continue to listen. We must know what he came so bravely to say to you." He put himself in jeopardy to communicate with you. But, now we know that King Forrest is still alive. It is not something many thought was possible. Please, let us resume watching."

Tremble started to question Laken further, but he seemed intent on resuming the dream. She wasn't exactly sure how to make it start again. She paused for a moment and looked at the face of her dear father. She wanted to have a moment to look at him, to remember his physical self in a healthy state. Hearing another voice come out of his mouth changed the experience entirely. She waved her hands in the same manner as before and the voice of Forrest resumed.

"He has no right to invoke the sin done to him onto a child from his future. Our loyal friends and comrades from the corners of most powerful regions of our universe have endeavored to learn of his whereabouts. Their efforts have been futile, but the knowledge they have gained has led us to one conclusion that I must share with you. Unlike our other ancestors who have been sentenced to a disembodied life within paintings, Scordato has full use of a physical body and can transport himself from place to place within our realm. It is not thought that he has the power to visit the human realm. We find this strange, but it may go back to a curse that was put on him by Perpetua. The curse binds him to his own world." The voice stopped for a moment. She watched, as her father appeared to be looking behind him.

"Did you know that?" Tremble used the lull to learn more from Laken.

"I knew of the curse. It is not known whether it prevents him from coming to the human world, or if it was a mere ploy by Perpetua to prevent Scordato from trying. I cannot imagine how King Forrest could know that for a certainty. He's talking again."

"Many in Neverwrong would disagree with what I am about to say. In fact, I daresay that all those who are your current guardians, including Laken, your Protector, will not agree with me in the slightest. But, none of them are your father. I will also be remiss if I do not tell you that your mother, Jasmine, also does not agree with me. Please listen carefully. As your father, it is my opinion that you should stay in the human world and not try to come to Neverwrong to confront Scordato. I realize that this will put our kingdom in jeopardy, but I think that it is time that I come forward and challenge Scordato to deal with me and me alone. I am the descendant of Baldric. It is my family line that caused him to be left behind. Your mother, naturally, thinks that she should join me in the effort. She also thinks that we should allow you to decide where you shall dwell and what you shall do. I do not agree. I will end this message now. Again, I apologize for using Andrew's physical likeness. It was not my intent, in any way, to be disrespectful to him. I hope it has not caused you unnecessary anguish. My heart has loved you above all others from the moment I was aware of your impending existence. I bid you a fond adieu and hope that someday I can hold my beautiful daughter in the security of her future."

The voice ceased and the image of her father disappeared. Tremble reached out to it, not knowing to who she was truly reaching for—the father she knew or the one she did not. Laken was silent, waiting for Tremble to speak.

"I think I would like to get dressed and ready for the day, if you don't mind."

"Certainly, I will leave you now. Perhaps we can talk about this later."

"I'm sure that you are going to want to discuss this with CeCe and Bridget."

"Actually, I was hoping that you might allow them to view it."

Tremble thought for a moment before she responded. "I'm not sure about that. I think once was enough for me."

"Very well, I understand. I will give them a report."

After Laken left, Tremble sat down on the bed and pulled a pillow to her chest. She then let out of her what had been growing inside since she first woke up. The tears came from the deepest part of her soul. She began to sob.

Chapter
Fifteen

"FLYING IS REALLY not as hard as it may sound."

After breakfast, Bridget and Laken began giving Tremble flying lessons.

"We do not have motorized vehicles in Neverwrong." Bridget had begun the lecture. "If you need to go somewhere, and it is farther than you can walk, you fly."

"Why don't you just will yourself to another place?" Tremble was trying to be attentive, but her mind was elsewhere.

"It is not a skill that everyone has the magic to carry out."

"It can also cause accidents when not used correctly." CeCe had been helping Dana in the kitchen. "Sometimes the caster is not as specific as needed and ends up somewhere he or she does not want to go."

"Flying is the best way."

"So are we talking broomsticks?"

Both Bridget and CeCe made a disgusted huffing sound. "Broomsticks. This human obsession with broomsticks. I blame that movie and every one since. And, don't anyone dare utter the name."

Tremble gave CeCe a questioning look. "Does Bridget mean?"

"Don't say it. It puts her off the deep end. I will give you a hint. Someone goes over the rainbow."

"Oh, I love that movie."

"Well, the overall premise is fine. But, its depiction of witches is horrendous." Bridget raised her arms up in the air to dramatically make her point. "Only bad witches are ugly and there is no kingdom where they are green. No, our dear Tremble, you do not need a broomstick to fly in Neverwrong or in any of the other magical kingdoms you may encounter. There is one thing that you definitely need though."

Laken stood up to demonstrate. "You need balance." Laken began to rise off of the ground.

"Most of the time you will need to be doing something else besides flying while you are in motion." CeCe rose and came up behind Laken. He quickly turned to protect himself. "For the most part we are a peaceful people. But, as in any culture, there are those who deviate and are aggressive. You have to be alert."

"Will I really be flying around Neverwrong very much?"

"Tremble, we really can't say what you will be doing." CeCe lowered herself to the ground as she spoke. Laken followed. "As much as we will try to take care of you, you will have to be able to take care of yourself, by yourself. Scordato is stronger than all of us. While we will do everything to prevent it, you may become separated from us at some point. We want you to be able to stand on your own, magically speaking."

"Listen to her, Tremble. I don't see how you can avoid a confrontation one day. You've got to be prepared."

Dana's words shocked Tremble. So much so that she decided to divulge her visit from Forrest.

"Oh, but there is an alternative, Mother. Has Laken told you of my visitor last night?"

CeCe and Bridget's expressions changed to concern. Dana did not seem to understand what Tremble was talking about.

"My father came to see me last night."

"Andrew? How is that possible?" Dana sank down into the nearest chair.

"Well, Mom, that's only partially correct. It was my biological father who came to visit. It was King Forrest. He visited me in a dream. He used the physical form of my father so that I would remember him."

Dana gasped. "I don't think I like that."

"That was my reaction at first. I understand though why he did it. He wanted me to remember the dream. I might not have remembered a dream with Forrest as his natural self. I do not know him."

"What did he want?" There was now an edge in Dana's voice.

"He had some information he wanted to share."

"Tremble, I really think that we should discuss this further before you share this information with your mother."

Laken suddenly seemed nervous and uncomfortable. The behavior made him look younger and weaker.

"I strongly disagree with that, young man." All semblance of friendly in Dana's voice was gone. "I think any discussions about Tremble should be done in front of me, period." Dana turned her attention back to her daughter. "What did he have to say?"

Tremble looked around the room before she began. No one

had a pleasant look.

"Basically, he wanted to tell me that there are many throughout the magical kingdoms who have unsuccessfully tried to find Scordato—that he is not confined to a painting like my other ancestors are. He also said that it is not believed that Scordato has the power to travel to the human world."

"Please remember that none of these things, especially Scordato's ability to travel, have been confirmed." Laken seemed to be priming the conversation for what Tremble might say next.

"Perhaps not, but I would tend to believe the one who has sacrificed his life for the last twenty years on Tremble's behalf." Dana nodded at Tremble, as she made her point. "Did he have anything else to say?" Dana paused, waiting for Tremble to answer. "Go ahead, tell me."

Tremble glanced at all three of her guardians. By the expressions on their faces, they all seemed to think they knew what she was going to reveal.

"Yes. He said that he had come once and touched my forehead while I was sleeping."

"That certainly seems like a dangerous thing for him to do. I can understand his parental longing to do so." Dana looked at the others. "Now, you may discuss this information among yourselves. I will be leaving in a few minutes to go shopping."

No one said a word after Dana left the room. Bridget and CeCe looked down at their coffee mugs. Laken just stared off into space. Tremble could imagine what was going through their minds. None of them probably had a clue that Forrest would make an appearance, let alone tell her to stay in the human world. It didn't seem like the type of thing he would do after going to such lengths to hide her. Tremble finally broke the silence.

"I really have nothing to base this on. It is merely an instinctual feeling." No one reacted. They were each in their own thought patterns. "I don't think it was Forrest. It may have been his voice, but I don't think they were entirely his words. It was like he was being coerced."

All three looked up simultaneously.

"What?" Laken was the first to respond.

"I think that someone forced him to do this."

"Have any of you ever talked with Forrest?"

"Yes, both Bridget and I have." CeCe spoke up. "We knew King Forrest before he went into hiding."

"Then perhaps I should conjure up that dream one more time and let you view it."

Tremble rose and walked toward the living room. The other three followed as she assumed the position and concentration necessary to extract the dream from her memory and into their view. Tremble found that this time was much easier. Bridget and CeCe were watching and listening intently when they heard a gasp.

"That is not my husband's voice. The voice does not belong there."

Tremble jumped up and ran toward her mother. Everything that had been in Dana's hands was now lying on the floor around her.

"I thought you had already left. I'm so sorry. It is supposed to be King Forrest's voice. I wanted them to hear it. Oh, Mom, I'm so sorry."

"He shouldn't be using your father." Dana tilted her head and walked closer to the screen. Tremble thought at first that she was going to reach out and touch it. "Oh, how I miss that face. He was still healthy then." Dana turned away and faced Tremble. She quickly wiped the tears that had begun to flow. "I am leaving now. You all get to the bottom of this. Tell that person he has no right to use my Andrew. I don't care who he is."

Bridget and CeCe continued to study the image and voice after Dana left. Every now and then they would look at each other. When it was over and the image had disappeared, Tremble felt exhausted, spent. She wasn't sure if it was the act of sharing her dream for view or the emotion attached to it.

"The voice is his. I have no doubt." CeCe stood up and began to pace. "The sound and the diction are quite precise. But, your instincts are correct, Tremble. It would be highly out of character for him to willingly risk visiting you this way."

"It is not consistent with King Forrest's behavior." Bridget joined CeCe in her pacing. "His background was in our military. He would not have willingly taken such a risk. He would not have conceded that Scordato was in some way justified by the actions that were done against him."

"At first, it passed through my mind that perhaps Scordato had captured Forrest and was forcing him to do this. But that doesn't make sense either. This whole thing about Scordato not being able to enter the human world is just preposterous. Even a commoner can come to this world. There is more difficulty returning to Neverwrong."

"Why is that?"

"Neverwrong is surrounded by what you might call a force field." Laken answered the question. "It is easy to get through it for departure. You have to have a certain level of magical strength and skill to return."

"This is why the celebrities that disappear in this world have trouble returning home. Most of them are commoners in Neverwrong. They have a lower level of magical skill. They always need assistance to return to Neverwrong." CeCe sat down and shook her head. "Scordato could blast holes through it. With the level of power we think he possesses, he could come and go multiple times a day if he wished."

"You may have just hit on something, CeCe." Bridget sat down next to her. "Maybe that really was Forrest's voice. Maybe Scordato captured him, and Forrest is trying to send us a message, a coded message. Maybe he has altered his manner to give us a clue. He wants to appear as if he was being limited in some manner."

CeCe and Bridget exchanged looks, before CeCe continued.

"Laken, you stay here with Tremble today and continue the discussion about our history. Maybe you all could go down to the beach later and practice flying. We are going to try to confer with Belladonna about this."

Laken looked like he wanted to object but seemed to think better of it. Tremble sensed that something wasn't quite right with him since he had returned.

"How can I practice flying with all the people who will be on the beach on a Saturday?"

Tremble was actually surprised that she knew what day it was. Time seemed to be a jumble since the day of the white jackets.

Bridget gave her a signature bubbly giggle as she walked by, patting Tremble on the shoulder.

"My dear, have you learned nothing from us so far? No one on the beach will actually be seeing you fly. Laken will make sure of that."

DANA HAD GONE shopping. CeCe and Bridget disappeared to try to communicate with Belladonna. Tremble left Laken downstairs so that she could take a shower and dress for a day on the beach. The shower had made her feel wonderful. So wonderful, she decided to crawl back into bed. Choo Choo made a similar comfortable place beside her. If she was lucky, Laken might leave her alone long enough so that she could have a quick nap and catch up on the previous night's interrupted sleep.

Tremble slid underneath the covers and closed her eyes. The relaxed feeling did not last long as she kept hearing a buzzing noise. This noise was definitely human technology in origin. It dawned on her that she had not seen her cell phone in, perhaps, a couple of days. She remembered putting it into her purse when they went out to dinner. Even then, she had been too distracted to open up the case. The thought made her realize how much her life had changed in a matter of a few days. Before, Tremble was always attentive to her phone.

Kicking the covers off her legs, she reached for her purse and began to dig through it. The multicolored leopard case was not hard to find. As she flipped it open, she was shocked to see all of the missed calls and text messages.

"Oh, gosh, VeVette, I forgot to call her."

Sure enough, seven of the eight voicemails were from her best friend. They started out lighthearted as she recounted the beach trip with her family. VeVette had two older brothers and each of them had four children. With her parents along, it meant that they had to rent a very large beach house. Tremble heard distress in VeVette's voice as she listened to the final two messages. Multiple text messages also conveyed her worry. Tremble debated whether to text or call. VeVette had the ability to detect that things were wrong with Tremble just by hearing her voice. She would be able to conceal more by sending a text message.

'Hey, VeVe. Your vacay sounded fab. Sorry I went AWOL.

Mom decided to take last minute trip to beach with couple of friends; she dragged me along. Not really, we are at the beach; I jumped at chance.'

Tremble hit 'send' and held her breath. Maybe VeVe would accept it without too much questioning. It did not take long for a response to return.

'You are so lucky that I did not tell my father, the policeman, about not hearing from you. I was so close. Glad you are soaking up some rays. How did you get time off from Cher and Bette?'

Tremble had told friend about the resemblances of her internship bosses to the famous ladies. VeVe had decided that those needed to be their code names. It seemed less comical now than it once had.

'They were cool when they heard it was my mother's trip. Have plenty of time to work. Thanks for being my friend, VeVe. Thanks for caring.'

For all that she knew now, it made her friendship with VeVe even more meaningful. To know that she was not someone who was planted in her life, but someone who had chosen her friendship and been true to it.

'You are stuck with me, Trem. No matter where you go, don't forget it. Text me tomorrow. Have fun. Hugs.'

'No matter where you go.'

Tremble sighed as she wondered if she would ever be able to tell VeVe where she was going.

The other voicemail was from Jake. He was apologizing all over himself again for showing up unannounced. He was pleading for her to just talk to him. Tremble hit 'delete.' How could he ever understand that he had probably been influenced to join the Navy? That a spell was put on him to assure that he left suddenly so he wouldn't be a distraction to her. He would never understand that she was from another world. She didn't understand it herself. He would be better off to never hear from her again.

All thoughts of rest were long gone. Tremble put on her bathing suit and a cover-up. She slipped on flip-flops as she began to walk down the stairs. She found Laken sitting stiffly in the living room viewing what appeared to be a shopping channel.

"Do humans really buy things from the television?"

Tremble smiled at the awkwardness of his word choice. "Yes, billions of dollars each year."

"I don't understand why humans buy things they do not even know if they need. They just see them and buy them. It is such a waste."

Tremble chuckled under her breath. He may not have lived in the human world, but he did have a unique understanding of human behavior.

"Okay, teacher, I am ready to learn. Let's make like Peter Pan and fly."

"What?"

Tremble's humor had flown right over Laken's head. "Let's go to the beach and you can teach me about the accepted mode of travel in Neverwrong." She didn't like the awkwardness in her own voice.

By the time the sun set that evening, Tremble had almost mastered the ability to fly for short periods. She had determined that the secret was not looking down.

"Laken tells me that you did quite well with your training." CeCe stood in the doorway of Tremble's room.

"It really wasn't as hard as I thought it would be." Tremble was sitting in one of the window seats reading.

"You should have some instinctual skills. Your ancestors have been flying for hundreds of years."

"CeCe, how am I supposed to process all of this? Everything that I have been told about Neverwrong and my heritage seems like it came straight out of a fantasy story."

"I was one of very few people who had the opportunity to talk to Jasmine about what she was going to do before she left to come to this world. She confided in me because of what would become my very close connection to Laken."

"Because you are Laken's aunt?"

"Because I gave birth to Laken."

"What?"

"I don't think that Bridget finished explaining to you about Laken. It's time you heard the rest of the story."

CeCe walked into the room and sat down in a beautiful rocking chair that was sitting in the corner of the room. Up until that point, Tremble had barely noticed the piece of furniture. It was unusual in its shape and size. It was lower to the ground than most rocking chairs were made and wider. Tremble wondered if it was actually a handmade piece of furniture that might have been from the personal collection of the owners of the house. It added personality to the room. It looked even larger with CeCe's svelte figure occupying it.

"I believe that Bridget has told you that Laken was created similarly to the test tube manner used in this world. The biology was simple. The egg came from someone in the Royal family. I do not know who that was. The sperm came from my brother, Anton. The embryo was created in a laboratory type environment. Belladonna was present and infused the embryo with a special blend of magic. So, it can be said that Laken truly has a bit of her within him as well. We suspect that Belladonna used an ancient spell in the process as she had spent an extensive amount of time alone in the mountains before the process took place."

"In the mountains? Do you think she was in the library you showed me? Does Scordato still control that space?"

"These are all good questions. Answering them is hard. Belladonna did not reveal where she went. Only her Protectors are aware of the exact location. Even then, she possesses the power to leave their physical presence and go places without them. I do not think that Belladonna has the power to physically enter the library. I do know that she and other Royals, including your mother, have had the power to mentally travel there and read select volumes."

"How is that possible?"

CeCe took a deep breath and paused. Her eyes were darting back and forth as if she was searching for something within her own mind.

"As you grow in your wisdom, understanding, and experience with magic, this concept will become clearer to you. As an enchantress, you can take many journeys within your own mind. Your mind can overcome the boundaries that a physical world puts up to block you. You can travel to places and experience many things without ever making a physical journey. I believe that Belladonna took an enchantress journey to find something very important to include in the special process that created Laken."

"I don't remember who has told me what, but someone said that the idea of Laken came to Jasmine in a dream."

"Yes, that is correct. She had a vision that her daughter was grown and that a young man was always with her. Apparently, there was something about this dream that told her that he would be a special Protector. I believe that Belladonna was the one who took this to heart. A test tube child had not been created in Neverwrong previously. Belladonna knew about it from her observances of the human news." Tremble gave her a confused look. "We get some of your channels in Neverwrong. Satellites serve many worlds." CeCe laughed and winked.

"Good to know. Bet you don't have the huge bills there."

"No, we do not. Money is a very different commodity there. But, that is indeed another story." CeCe rocked back and forth for a few minutes. She seemed to be pondering what she would next divulge. "Laken is the only being from Neverwrong to have been created in this manner. I was his surrogate mother. His birth was timed to occur on the same day as yours. You two share a birthday." Tremble noticed that CeCe touched her stomach as she said these words.

"Timed?"

"He was taken by cesarean."

"Wow, CeCe. I don't know what to say. That must have been hard."

"Well, Tremble. It was complicated. Even though a mortal surrogate mother does not have a genetic link to the child, her health is crucial to the growth of the fetus. It's a little different with an immortal surrogate. Actually, I am the only immortal surrogate that we know that has existed."

"What makes it different?"

"It is thought that the immortal surrogate, the magical surrogate, will bestow some of her powers onto the child. In this case, additionally, Belladonna used a spell to impart some special abilities onto Laken." CeCe looked Tremble straight in the eyes. "Please understand, I was honored to do this. I have not been Laken's mother in the conventional sense. I have had the opportunity though to be a key person in his life. He knows of our relationship and he understands it." CeCe laughed. "Sometimes I think he is extra defiant with me because of it. As a son might be under traditional circumstances."

"How do you think Laken feels about the reasons behind his birth?"

"That is a very compassionate question, Tremble. I'm glad that you asked it. Laken went through a period of time a few years ago where he challenged the decisions that were made for him. It wasn't that he didn't want to do any of this. Laken has been very devoted to you since he was very young. He knew there was a connection early on. He began to challenge why he couldn't make some of his own decisions. This was after his father died and that strong male role model was missing. Even at that young age, Laken had a level of maturity and responsibility. He made some valid points. Belladonna listened and allowed him to make some of his own decisions."

"Like what?"

"Well, he thought it would be beneficial if he served a couple of years in the Neverwrong Army. He went through the whole experience, from training to service, without any special considerations by the Royal family. He even served for six months in the deserts of Morbathia. It is an extremely remote area. Some do not survive assignments to that area."

"That's interesting, and brave. There's something else though about his personality. He just seems so stiff and serious."

CeCe stood up and began walking toward the doorway. "I don't think you have judged that quite right, my dear. I think he's nervous. I believe that finally being in the presence of his beautiful charge has been a little more disconcerting than he thought. All through his growing up years, we have shown him photos as well as allowed him to hear your voice and see glimpses of you in action. While you have been in college, he has been in the Army. You've changed from an awkward teenager to a self-assured young woman. We've noticed. So has he." CeCe gave Tremble a wink.

"Wait, CeCe, you didn't tell me what Belladonna said about the message from Forrest."

"Well, Tremble, there isn't much that she could say. No one has heard from King Forrest for a very long time. Many Protectors have thought that he might have perished. Some of us, including Belladonna, haven't given up hope. We know one thing for certain. Scordato doesn't really want to harm Jasmine or Forrest. In fact, you might say that he is probably happy that they have helped put the prophecy in motion. Scordato has waited hundreds of years for this. If he has your father, he will not harm him. At least not until he has the opportunity to see what you will do."

"So, it all comes down to me."

"I'm afraid it does, my dear. Take heart. You have many helpers." CeCe smiled, as she closed the door behind her.

Chapter
Sixteen

SPELLS. TREMBLE'S HEAD was full of spells. From early morning until late evening, Laken, CeCe, and Bridget took turns teaching the long and short, easy and complicated incantations to their student.

"It's like cramming for finals without having taken the class." Tremble ran her fingers through her bedhead of hair and small bolts of light crackled around her.

"You need to shake off the spell, as we showed you, before you do that. You are going to catch your hair on fire." Laken chuckled and shook his head.

"Well, excuse me, Professor, I've only been doing this for a week or so. Why don't you teach me a spell to put my hair out?"

"I'm merely trying to warn you about the consequences." Laken started to walk away. "And I did teach you that." He mumbled to himself.

"You know, you are really getting on my nerves."

"Okay, you two, simmer down." CeCe walked between them as Tremble rose to follow him. "Everyone is tired and on edge. I know we have given you way too much to grasp. You've worked hard. I think you have enough of the basics for now. It's only ten o'clock. Why don't we take a break and resume after lunch? Laken, I think it would be appropriate for this, our last afternoon here, that you plan to continue with your overview of Never-wrong history."

Laken nodded and gave Tremble a stern stare. It made her want to stick her tongue out at him.

"After that, Bridget and I are going to spend this evening telling you more details about Jasmine. It is time that you learn who the wonderful woman is who gave you life."

Tremble nodded and left the room. As she passed the kitchen area, she saw her mother standing at the counter chopping vegetables. She paused and studied her. The trip had relaxed Dana in some ways. Her mother had spent several afternoons sunbathing on the beach. A bronze tan had replaced the pallor to her mother's skin. Dana was an easy tanner, but life hadn't presented too many opportunities in recent years for her to bask in the sun's heat. Despite the relaxation, there was a worry that seemed to hang on her shoulders. Tremble knew that the time would soon come for her to venture out into this new world she had been learning about. She worried that the separation would be a constant source of concern for her mother. She hoped that CeCe and Bridget had ways of lessoning the burden.

She walked into the kitchen and gave her mother a quick hug. Grabbing a couple of small pieces of cheese from the fridge, she also picked up an apple and a bottle of water before she headed up stairs.

"Recess from spell school?"

Tremble loved her mother's sarcasm. It was one of the personality traits that bonded them. Tremble now knew that this commonality was more nurture than nature.

"Yes, I'm going to go upstairs and rest a little. I might try to get in a run before lunch if it isn't sweltering."

Choo Choo wagged her tail in excitement as she heard Tremble say run. For the most part, Dana had been taking care of her since they arrived.

"Come on up and nap with me, and then we will go run."

As Tremble began to eat her snack, she heard her cell phone vibrate on the nightstand. It was Jake. She started to ignore it, but she took a deep breath and answered.

"Hello."

"Hey, Tremble. I expected to get your voicemail. This is Jake. How are you?"

"Hi, Jake. I'm fine."

"Well, my leave is about over and I will be heading back to the base soon. I was wondering if maybe we could get together."

"Thanks for asking. But, I am out of town right now."

"Oh."

Tremble could hear the disappointment in his voice.

"I'm with Mom and some of her friends. We are at the beach."

"Oh, well, that sounds great. I hope you are having a good time."

"It's a lot like—" Tremble almost said 'work,' but caught herself. "Mom needed some time away."

"Yeah, sure. Well, I guess that's that."

There was a long pause.

"Jake, I appreciate you calling. It's probably best if we just say goodbye."

"Tremble, I messed up. I know I messed up bad. I can't explain it. I don't know what I was thinking. It's like one minute I was filling out college applications and learning about fraternities, and the next minute I was getting a buzz cut and dressing in fatigues. It's like I blacked out and woke up with a new life."

Tremble's heart broke all over again. Now she knew a spell was cast on Jake. Someone in Neverwrong's legion of Protectors had decided that he shouldn't be her boyfriend anymore. She was hurt and angry and scared. She would get to the bottom of this. Someone had some serious explaining to do.

"Jake, don't beat yourself up about it. We're young. We make reckless decisions."

"I know I have waited too long to even think that you might—"

"Life is very busy and confusing right now." Those might have been the truest words Tremble would say in the whole conversation. "I really don't think it is a good time to revisit the past. You make sure that you call me next time you come home to visit your folks." Tremble held her breath.

"Yeah, I understand." Jake paused and cleared his throat. "I wish with all my heart that I hadn't been such an idiot. I remember telling you on the night I first kissed you that I would always be there for you."

"You would slay a dragon for me." The memory jumped out of Tremble's mouth before she could stop it.

"Yeah, silly words from a kid. But, I meant them. I promised your dad that I would always protect you. When he was dying, I told him that I would be your protector."

The statement slapped Tremble in the face.

"He never told me that." Her voice had become a whisper. Anger began to brew inside her that would be hard to contain.

"Well, you know, it was a man-to-man thing." Jake chuckled nervously. "I understand if you have moved on with your life, if you have someone else. There was probably a long line of guys waiting to take my place." Tremble was silent. "Only, I was hoping I could get in line."

Tremble laughed, but she was choking back tears. Jake really loved her. Now that the spell had worn off, he could tell her the truth.

"Oh, Jake. It's complicated." She bit her lip. She couldn't lie to him. "It isn't someone else. My life isn't exactly my own right now. I really can't explain. You will just have to trust me."

"Soooo, will your life be yours by Christmas?"

Through the phone line she could almost see him pacing. His left hand on his cell phone, his right hand trying to make a point. Then, the same hand would run through his hair. It helped him think. But, that hair was long gone, courtesy of the United States Navy. His life wasn't his own either.

"Are you going overseas, Jake?" The thought occurred to her that his leave time seemed long. Perhaps, it was because he was going to be sent on a long assignment. There was silence on his side of the conversation. "Jake?"

"Yes, I wasn't planning on telling you that." Tremble could hear him take a deep breath. She opted to hold hers. "I'm going to the Middle East. I've done well in training. They assigned me to work in Intelligence on this mission. It's an incredible opportunity for me to advance quickly."

Excelling was nothing new to Jake. His high school sports career was the type that movies were made about. College recruiters had been drooling since he was a sophomore. It was one of the things that shocked her the most when he enlisted. But, he wasn't just a jock. Academically, he excelled as well, and had a special strength in mathematics and computer software language. She expected him to pursue a future in IT; she never imagined he would go overseas.

"Wow, Jake, that's serious."

"Yeah, a little. I won't be exactly on the front line, just close to it." Tremble could hear a nervous laugh under his breath. "I guess that is part of the reason I wanted to spend a little time with you. I don't know when I will get leave again. I will probably be deployed for at least a year."

How many days had she known about her real heritage? Tremble couldn't even remember, ten, maybe. Everything in her life had changed so much. Even with all of the unimaginable shock of this immortal life of hers, she also would have never imagined that she would be having this conversation with Jake. Her heart had closed the door to him. She had put him in a box and stored him away where her feelings could not resurface.

"I understand if you don't want to. My timing is bad with you being out of town and all."

Tremble's mind raced. With all the uncertainty of her immediate and long-term future, she didn't want to have regrets.

"When do you have to leave? We're going home tomorrow. Tomorrow is Wednesday, isn't it?" Tremble wasn't quite sure, but thought they had been at the beach for about a week.

"Yes, I have to leave on Friday. Does that mean you might agree to see me?"

Her mind said no, but her heart said yes. It was the right thing to do. Even if it was goodbye. They both deserved that.

"Yes, let's tentatively plan to spend some time together on Thursday. I will text you when we get home tomorrow."

"Oh, Tremble, that would be fabulous."

"Jake, we will have a nice dinner and catch up. Don't read too much into this. Neither one of us needs any more complications right now, agreed?"

"Yes." There was silence for a few moments. "I appreciate you taking the time."

"It will be good to see you again, Jake. I'll text you tomorrow."

Tremble set her phone back on the nightstand. She let her mind wander to her memories of Jake. There were many good memories, many special times. She felt the nuzzling of Choo Choo's nose on her back, reminding her of the promise she had made to her furry friend.

"It's time we go for a run, little girl. Then, Mommy is going to come back and put the fear of God into her Protector."

"I DON'T CARE if it doesn't fit into the great plan for Neverwrong. This is my life and you do not have permission to make decisions for me."

Tremble waited until they had finished eating lunch before she confronted Laken. Her run had worked considerably to give her some control, but she would have to run all the way to Neverwrong to extinguish the anger she felt over what had been done to Jake.

"My whole purpose revolves around your protection." Laken's tone was unusually smug. He seemed a little angry as well. His aura was green, a deepening green.

"I do not need to be protected from Jake."

Tremble glanced around the table and saw that all three of the others were intently watching the interaction between them. None of them said a word. She thought she saw that her mother was trying to hide a slight smile.

"I think his behavior says otherwise."

"The behavior that was caused by the spell you put on him." Tremble could feel her blood pressure rising.

"Now, Tremble, I don't think you can blame Laken for Jake running off like he did. Jake made that decision himself." Dana furrowed her brow as she made her comment.

"Oh, you don't think I should blame Laken, do you? Let's ask him."

All eyes went to Laken. He looked uncomfortable. Tremble thought she saw the beginnings of him turning colors again.

"Well, Mr. Protector, did you or did you not put a spell on my boyfriend to influence him to join the Navy?"

Laken darted his eyes at CeCe and Bridget. His square jaw clinched.

"Laken, you didn't?" CeCe did not look very happy. "You know that is against protocol."

"There must have been some other threatening behavior that we don't know about." Bridget jumped into the conversation. "Did you learn something about Jake that made you concerned for Tremble's safety?"

All eyes went back to Laken. His neck was red. Tremble thought she saw beads of sweat forming on his temples.

"Not exactly."

"Laken, what have you done?"

Knowing now what Tremble did about CeCe's part in Laken's birth gave the whole scenario she was watching a new meaning. CeCe did have somewhat of a motherly tone when she spoke to Laken. Tremble had not noticed it previously.

"He was going to be a distraction."

"A distraction?" Dana's voice indicated that she did not like what she was hearing. "Jake had been a part of Tremble's life for several years at that point. Andrew and I never worried in the slightest about his influence on Tremble. In fact, I was very saddened when he left suddenly. It seemed so out of character for him." Realizing what she had said, Dana reached over and squeezed Tremble's hand. "I had no idea."

"I was prepared to become her Protector two years ago. I thought that all would have been revealed before now." Laken gave a pleading look in Bridget's direction. She just shook her head. "She didn't need him to be distracting her from her future."

Bridget was sitting on the other side of Tremble. She reached out and took hold of her other hand. "Try to remain calm, Tremble."

"Oh, I'm calm. Don't worry about me. There's been an almost hour run on the beach with Choo Choo and some of my mother's cooking between my learning this information and now." Tremble gave Bridget a big fake toothy grin. "Laken is just very fortunate that no one has taught me any termination spells."

"Tremble, those are strong words." Dana squeezed her hand and cut her eyes to her daughter. "What is it that you now know about this situation? How do you know it?"

"Jake called while I was upstairs resting. I answered." Tremble thought she heard her mother catch her breath. "Jake was apologizing all over himself. I thought at first it was him having regrets. Then he said this." In a flash, Tremble extracted the conversation from her memory. No chanting needed, it was a reflex, and she didn't even know it.

Unlike the dream, there was no image, but clear as day was Jake's voice. 'Tremble, I messed up. I know I messed up bad. I can't explain it. I don't know what I was thinking. It's like one minute I was filling out college applications and learning about fraternities and the next minute I was getting a buzz cut and dressing in fatigues. It's like I blacked out and woke up with a new life.'

"How did you know how to do that?" Laken's shocked look surprised Tremble.

"Don't try to change the subject." Tremble pushed herself away from the table and stood up. She looked Laken in the eye. "You put a spell on Jake and changed my life. Your assignment as my Protector does not give you the right to do that, not in my book." Tremble turned to leave the room, but changed her mind.

"I will continue with my training, with this mission of my heritage. I will do it because I have two mortal parents who sacrificed for me and raised me not to shirk from my responsibilities. I will do it because my immortal parents have banished themselves from their own lives so that I could safely grow to adulthood."

Tremble turned and looked straight at Laken, CeCe, and Bridget.

"But, from now on, I call the shots on my life. None of you, or Belladonna, will dictate who is in my life or how it proceeds. You will advise. You will teach. You will guide. You will protect. Tremble will decide. I will be back downstairs in an hour for my Neverwrong history lesson by Laken. Bridget and CeCe, I look forward to hearing more about Jasmine after dinner. We're going home in the morning."

TREMBLE WAS SILENT as she entered the living room. Laken was sitting in a straight back chair looking solemn.

"Proceed with your history lesson."

"Tremble, I'm sorry if I was out of line. It's my responsibility to protect you from anything or anyone who might hinder—"

"Proceed with your history lesson, Laken."

Laken lost eye contact with Tremble. With a flick of his wrist, a screen appeared for their view. It showed a circular room with seven portrait paintings. The subjects of the paintings looked regal and distinguished.

"For many decades, the history of the Kingdom of Neverwrong told the story of seven siblings who ventured out of a faraway mountain and came to be the first rulers of our kingdom. It was not until much later that it was revealed to the general citizens of Neverwrong that an eighth sibling also existed. The revelation of this other sibling and how he came to be the forgotten one was a source of pain and embarrassment for Queen Perpetua and her sisters. It was a source of anger and frustration for King Baldric."

"How was Scordato's existence hidden for all of those years? I saw that The Seven discovered he was alive when they were still in their youth. The wise one you spoke of previously, the oldest being in Neverwrong, I can't remember his name, he knew about Scordato, didn't he?"

"Meserve. Yes, he knew of him. Meserve prophesied about what the evil force would do." An image of a man came on the screen. Tremble gasped. She had never seen someone so old looking.

"Is that Meserve?"

"Yes, it is. Meserve has an important role in the history of Neverwrong. His true connection to the Royal Family, however, is steeped in secrecy. What we know for a certainty is that he has always been fiercely loyal to all of the Royal family."

"So, he's still alive?"

"Yes, we believe so. He has not been seen for many years though. We fear that he could be held by Scordato. He is the keeper of the prophecy. He is the one that prophesied that the union of two of the lines of The Seven would result in, for the first time, a female being the firstborn of Baldric's line."

"So, if I had been a boy, the prophecy would not have been fulfilled?"

"No. But, it was going to happen, sooner or later."

"Lucky me. It's now."

"I hope that Neverwrong is the lucky one. Lucky that it is you."

Tremble paused and thought about what Laken had said. It was a sobering responsibility to hold the future of a world in an unexperienced grasp.

"Continue with your history lesson."

Laken repeated aspects that Tremble already knew, such as the names of the sisters and the dividing of the territory. She knew that she needed to learn the basics of the family tree, but her eyes started glazing over as Laken recounted around a hundred years of branches.

"Most scholars of Neverwrong history agree that, up until now, the most important time period in our history was when The Seven made the decision to bestow magical powers on their subjects."

"I thought it was Queen Perpetua who did that."

Tremble was pleased that Laken finally honed in on a topic that interested her. Dana was baking cookies for the return trip and the smell was very distracting.

"It was Queen Perpetua's idea. All seven had to be in agreement in order for the spell to work."

"Baldric agreed to it? That's a little surprising based on the character you have painted him to be."

"As I said earlier, the commoners did not know about Scordato and the prophecy, at that time. It would have been very difficult for Baldric to establish his rule with such an embarrassment over his head. Perpetua used that as a bargaining tool with him. He agreed to participate in the spell, and she agreed to keep his indiscretion regarding their brother a secret for as long as possible."

Laken excused himself for a moment, and Tremble used that time to sort out some of what he had told her. By the time he returned, she had questions.

"Did he ever own up to leaving his brother to die? Surely that was a mistake on his part."

"That I am aware of, Baldric never publicly acknowledged that it was intentional. But, Belladonna says that a conversation occurred shortly after The Seven's return from the mountain between Baldric, Perpetua, and Abelia ended with Baldric crumbling to the ground and begging for his sisters' forgiveness. He claimed jealousy and the folly of youth. Some of his actions later in his life might lead one to believe that this youthful behavior was not isolated to that time period. Baldric was, in many regards, a hard man. One could also speculate that finding out his brother had actually lived might have contributed to his later personality and actions."

"Great. Quite a bag of DNA I have inherited."

"As much as that plays into your development, I would say that Andrew and Dana have had an equal or greater influence. I have no worries as to the type of person you are." Laken paused. "But, I don't want to cross you either."

Tremble saw a smug look cross Laken's face. She mirrored the look on her own.

"Then you better not mess with my love life again."

"I am your Protector. I wanted to protect. I know I overstepped my bounds. I only want what is best for you. You should have someone in your life who is devoted to you. Jake was always distracted with sports. You need devotion."

"It's my choice, no one else's. Devotion can lead to dangerous things sometimes." Tremble heard in her own voice the concern that she knew was in her heart. This young man in front of her had a dangerous level of devotion.

FOR THEIR FINAL evening at the beach, they had decided to again find a seaside restaurant to enjoy a relaxing meal. Although their time was limited, Tremble had relished the easygoing ocean lifestyle.

"Laken, you use these cracker thingies to crack open the crab legs."

Bridget was giving Laken a lesson in how to properly eat crab legs. Heaping plates of the seafood had already come and gone from their table. Tremble was dying to snap a photo of him and Bridget in their tacky bibs.

"When we return to your home, things are going to be very different." CeCe's comment changed the mood of the table.

"What do you mean? Has something happened to our house?" Dana looked up from the plate of oysters she was eating.

"Oh, no, nothing like that. Our security on Tremble will tighten. Bridget and I will probably disband Kaleidoscope, and—"

"What? Why? Kaleidoscope is a phenomenal company. You have so many clients. You employ lots of people." Tremble could not believe what she was hearing.

"That is correct. But, the company only exists because we wanted a good cover and something interesting to do while you were growing up."

"You can't disband your company. What about when all of this is over?"

"We will go back to live in Neverwrong. We will have another assignment." CeCe looked at Bridget; she had a faraway look in her eyes. "Won't we?"

"Tremble may have a point. Closing the company may be hasty. Tremble might even want to take it over later."

"Tremble will be the Supreme Ruler of Neverwrong." Laken jumped into the conversation.

"Tremble is sitting in the room." The relaxed feeling was leaving Tremble very quickly. "If I am successful in whatever this mission will present, I am not sure that I will want to spend the rest of my life in Neverwrong. This is my home." Tremble looked at Dana. "I can't imagine not living here, at least some of the time. Besides, if I am the Supreme Ruler, as you say, I should be able to do whatever I want."

Everyone around the table smiled, except Laken. His handsome exterior was compromised by a look of disgust.

"Queen Jasmine would not have such a reaction. I am sure that she longs for the opportunity to return to her homeland."

"Well, I am sure that you are correct about that. I know little about what Jasmine would do. I thought that CeCe and Bridget were going to tell me about her this evening."

"I suggest that we hold that thought until we have finished our meal and are back at the beach house."

Tremble gave her mother a look of displeasure. She knew that those around them could not hear what they were really saying.

"Dana is right." CeCe intervened. "Let's finish our entrees and get some luscious dessert to go. It will be better to have this conversation in a more relaxing environment."

"LIKE MANY OF those close to her, Jasmine was born into extreme opulence." And, so it began, the conversation that would change Tremble's life. CeCe was the first to speak. "A Royal child of Neverwrong wants for nothing. Privilege and protection are showered upon such a child. Education is of great importance, especially to the children in the lineage of Perpetua. As the first-born in her family, Jasmine was groomed to one day ascend to the throne. While she took her royal legacy seriously, it was not the center of her existence. Jasmine yearned for more."

"The story is told that when Jasmine was twelve years old, she, Belladonna, and Forrest were having a day of exploration within the woodland area that borders the City of Tristeza." Bridget took over the story. "Despite her sister's cautions, Belladonna began climbing a very high tree. Belladonna was nine, at the time, and had quite the streak of tomboy in her."

"Anton was the cause of that." CeCe chimed in. "They were already very close playmates. She wanted to do everything he did."

Tremble noticed a tinge of sadness to CeCe's smile as she mentioned her brother's name.

"Belladonna fell from a high limb and broke her arm. It was then that Jasmine's healing talents were revealed. Forrest later said that it was as if she created her own spell as she witnessed her sister's pain and immediately mended the bone."

"From then on, Jasmine focused on developing her gift. Even though most young women of her position were not encouraged to develop a trade, so to speak, Jasmine's parents were supportive of her increasing her skills."

"History tells us that Jasmine is the most powerful healer since Perpetua." Laken had remained silent up until that point. "In the Letters of Perpetua, she hints to a guilt that she carried regarding the healing of someone in her family by the slightest touch of her hand. At the time, she did not realize she possessed such power. Some have speculated that perhaps Amadeus was actually dead or very near it when he was put into the box in the Library, and that Perpetua's touch before it was closed began a healing that was not complete until later."

"Oh my, that is a twisted tale." Dana scowled and shook her head. "There are so many layers to that story."

"Isn't there some way to go back and view that time as we did when The Seven found their brother?"

"That is an excellent question, Tremble." CeCe accepted the cup of coffee that Dana handed her. They had returned to the beach house from the restaurant with elaborate desserts. "Unfortunately, what happened to Amadeus after his siblings left is only in *his* memory."

"I don't understand. How were we able to view what we did?"

"Ah, we failed to explain that part of the equation." Laken poured several spoons of sugar into his coffee as he spoke. Tremble suppressed a giggle as she watched him. "Once The Seven left their physical lives and began inhabiting the Royal paintings, they agreed to allow a complicated spell to be cast that would allow for the use of their memories by others. It was hoped that future generations would be able to use the information to help overthrow Scordato when the time came."

"And, of course, Scordato is still a physical being and has not agreed to such."

"Precisely." Bridget took a bite of a sizable piece of mandarin coconut cake. "Oh, Dana, you have got to try this. The frosting is scrumptious."

Tremble sipped her second cup of coffee as she pondered what she had just been told. An uneaten slice of apple pie sat before her.

"Has anyone had any encounters with Scordato in recent times?"

CeCe, Bridget, and Laken all stopped eating and looked at each other.

"What did I say?"

"What has made you ask that?" CeCe was the first to speak.

"Well, I was just thinking that perhaps if someone met him face-to-face, the person might be able to somehow work a spell to get into his memory. That may be farfetched, but magic does seem to be able to overcome some fairly sizable barriers."

"Did you tell her something?" CeCe questioned Laken. "You know that you were not supposed to divulge—"

"Absolutely not. We never even got near this topic."

"So, Tremble's magical mind is farther advanced than we suspected." A big smile crossed Bridget's face. "I daresay that with a little coaching she might be able to crack that nut, humanly speaking." Bridget released a nervous giggle as her eyes darted around in search of some fragment of knowledge.

"I have no doubt that Tremble has the magical genetics to do it if anyone ever could have. But, she would still have to be physically in the same room with him." CeCe's eyes were darting back and forth as well. Only Laken was staring straight ahead.

"That is a danger that she is not ready—"

"Wait a minute. Tremble is again in the room. Can you please stop talking about me like I am not here?"

"But, she might be able to summon him." All eyes went to Laken. "Remember, besides healing, that is one of Jasmine's most pronounced powers. Forrest is legendary in his military career for his ability to find enemies in hiding. It is why some feel that he was captured by Scordato. Forrest might have really found him."

"Tremble can find anything that is lost." Everyone looked at Dana. "Really, it's true. Since she was a baby, if Andrew or I were looking for something in the house, all we had to do was mention it to her and she would find it. It even applied to things that were boxed away that she had no knowledge regarding. It's like she has radar."

"Oh, Mom, I just kept looking. Most people get frustrated and stop."

"No, Tremble, you can find anything. You two remember when the little girl went missing from Tremble's elementary school." CeCe and Bridget thought for a moment, and then their eyes got big with realization. "Andrew and I told Tremble about it. We showed her a photo of the little girl. Her name was Shelley. We knew it was risky, but it was a missing child. We had to see if it might work." CeCe and Bridget nodded. "Do you remember any of this?"

"No, I have no idea what you are talking about." Tremble furrowed her brow and shook her head.

"It was removed from your memory."

"How nice. It's a wonder that I have any memories at all."

"Tremble."

"Just saying what I think, Mom. I guess everyone should get used to that." Tremble dived into the apple pie with a vengeance.

"So, did I find the little girl?" There was silence. Tremble looked up from her plate. Her mother's look was stern.

"Yes, you did."

"Great, happy ending. So what does this have to do with Scordato?"

"It wasn't a happy ending. You found her. It was too late."

"Too late for what?"

"She was dead, Tremble." CeCe answered the question. "The little girl had been abducted. You described how to find her, where she was. When the police arrived, it was too late. Not every story has a happy ending."

Tremble sat in silence as, one by one, everyone began leaving the room. Her mother was the last to leave.

"We knew that they could remove that from your memory. We never allowed you to do anything like that again. From then on, we only let you find the car keys." Dana smiled as she kissed Tremble on the forehead.

"Do you think I could find him?"

"Scordato?"

"Yes. Could I find the black sheep of the family?" Tremble scoffed at her own joke. "How did I do it?"

"What do you mean?"

"When I found something, when I found that little girl— how did I do it?"

"I'm really not sure. But, I do remember that you took the photograph in your hand and you stared at it for quite a long time. Then, you stared in front of you. Your eyes darted back in forth like you were seeing something. In the years since, I've noticed that same eye movement. It's like you are seeing an object or following it with your eyes."

"Well, that might be a little harder with Scordato."

"Indeed it would." Dana began to leave the room. Right before she reached the doorway, she turned back. "You said something earlier about there being an alternative. Something that Forrest had mentioned. Do you want to share that with me?"

"He said that I should just stay here in this world and let him and Jasmine deal with Scordato."

"That would be a wonderful alternative."

"But?"

"But, as much as your mother in this world would love it, it is not the way this prophecy is supposed to play out. You are the heir to Neverwrong. It is your responsibility. Your father and I didn't raise you to run away from your responsibilities. I can't help but think about what we've heard about how Queen Perpetua named the kingdom—you are never wrong when you do what is right. That is your destiny."

"It's a beautiful day for travelling." Bridget passed a plate of French toast to Laken. "Traffic shouldn't be too bad."

Everyone had arisen early for the final morning at the beach. CeCe had been practicing yoga on the deck. Bridget and Dana were packing and making breakfast. Tremble took a long run while Laken entertained Choo Choo and looked for seashells. No one spoke of Neverwrong or the reasons they were all together. Breakfast was served on the deck so they could soak up a little more relaxing sunshine before departure.

"I don't think you finished telling me about Jasmine. I guess my abruptness ended the conversation." Tremble absentmindedly danced a strawberry with her fork in a sea of maple syrup. "I apologize for that. Sometimes what you have to tell me is more than I can handle hearing."

"We understand, Tremble. Unfortunately, it will get worse before it gets better." CeCe reached over and squeezed Tremble's hand. "Talking about your dear mother is one of our favorite topics. The people of Neverwrong wake up every morning hoping that it will be the day that Queen Jasmine returns to them. It will happen. We feel certain. Her reign shall be long and happy. If we can ever rid this universe of Scordato and the evil that controls him."

"We told you a little yesterday about her healing powers. Only Jasmine's immediate family and the Protectors who accompanied her know of the secret missions she took to this world and others to help people during some very turbulent times of illness."

Bridget waved her hand and a screen appeared. It showed a black and white image that seemed very strange to Tremble as all of the other images she had seen that way were in vivid color.

"There are few enchanters who can travel back in time. You would think that would be a common ability for someone with magical powers. Interestingly, it is more common for a mortal to be able to time travel. When the ability shows up in an immortal, it usually indicates that there was a human long ago in their lineage."

"You mean, I'm not completely immortal? Trust me; it would be good news to me." Tremble gave thumbs up to Dana. Her mother was on her third cup of coffee.

"I think we need more coffee."

Dana began to gather the breakfast dishes. Laken jumped up to help her, gaining a smile from Dana.

"Well, we do not know for certain. But, considering Jasmine's special ability, it is very likely that there was at least a drop of mortal to her lineage." CeCe rejoined the conversation. "What is interesting about the story that Bridget has begun to tell you is that Jasmine was so intent on helping people that she risked her very existence doing something that no one else in her family could do. At least three times during her late teens and early twenties, Jasmine took trips back in time to help lessen massive outbreaks of disease. This photo is from the 1918 influenza epidemic that infected over five hundred million humans around this world. It has been speculated that between fifty and one hundred million people died. It was one of the deadliest natural disasters in human history." The photo changed as many other somber ones flashed quickly across the screen before returning to the original photo. "See the woman in the background?"

As Tremble looked closely at the old photograph, another photo was placed beside it. It was a headshot of a young Jasmine, also in black and white for comparison.

"Wow, that's amazing. So what did Jasmine do to help?"

"A study of human history told Jasmine that two of the primary factors that contributed to the pandemic's severity was the fast spread of the disease, possibly because of increased means of transportation in that era, and pneumonia. Jasmine travelled around the world to some of the areas that were the most severely hit and encouraged doctors to practice strict quarantines and to more aggressively treat the pneumonia symptoms as they developed. She knew that this would not completely eradicate the disease, but that it would help curb some of the fatalities."

"Jasmine used her magical means of transportation to get her from one part of the globe to another." Bridget stepped back into view. "This was a very risky thing to do while time travelling."

"So, some of these doctors actually listened to her?"

"As I believe your mother mentioned several days ago, Jasmine could be very convincing. She has a way of getting others to trust her and believe her quickly and completely."

"That is just amazing. It makes me feel really good about her."

"That it should." Bridget paused for a moment before continuing. "Another one of her journeys took her back over one thousand years to the Kingdom of Mercy."

"Where is that?"

Laken had rejoined them and spoke up to answer the question. "Mercy was another parallel reality to this world. It predates Neverwrong. Unfortunately, those who Jasmine tried to help did not listen. The entire population of Mercy perished from the dehydration."

"You are just a history book of knowledge, aren't you?" Laken gave Tremble a confused look after her comment. "You just don't know if I am being sarcastic or mean, do you?"

"None of us do, Tremble. May we continue?" Bridget shook her head. "As Laken said, the entire population of Mercy died from dehydration. Try as she might, Jasmine could not get them to understand that, like humans, the inhabitants of Mercy needed to drink water. It does not have to be something complicated to take out a civilization if they refuse to help themselves."

"There are other examples that show the depths of her compassion for others, especially strangers. Even before she made the daring step of marrying your father and the selfless act of giving you a protected life away from her, Jasmine was someone who we all admired and respected." Bridget nodded and removed the screen as CeCe concluded her thoughts. "We expect no less from you, my dear."

Tremble looked up and saw her mother walking back onto

the deck. Dana stopped when they made eye contact. For a moment, Tremble actually felt that her mother was reading her thoughts. Dana gave her a brief smile and shook her head encouragingly. Tremble stood up and took a deep breath.

"Well, I appreciate everything that each of you has taught me. I know that there will be a lot more for me to learn. But, it sounds like it is time for me to go and find Jasmine."

CeCe and Bridget smiled and shook their heads. Laken stood up and started to speak, but not before Tremble continued.

"But, first, I've got to go home and have a date with Jake." Before any of them could blink, Tremble disappeared.

A few moments later, she appeared in front of her mother on the other side of the room. CeCe and Bridget clapped as they saw she had reappeared. Trembled winked at her mother as she linked her arm through hers and they began to walk back inside. She glanced back over her shoulder and saw Laken sink back into his chair. Choo Choo jumped up on his lap and began to lick his face.

"Now, that was fun." Tremble laughed. "I think I just might be able to handle this."

ACKNOWLEDGEMENTS

Unless it is your intention to live a solitary life, you must carefully choose a few people along the way to take your journey with you. Writing a novel, a series, is no different. In this case though, I was blessed to have with me on this magical journey, some very enchanting people. It is with humble appreciation that I now bestow my thanks.

A writer's best friend is her editor. I'm fortunate that my main editor for this series was indeed one of my dearest friends. Pam Newberry graciously took time away from her own writing pursuits (check them out at www.pambnewberry.com) to be the voice of reason for my words' earliest drafts. Her ability to simultaneous be an editor and reader by asking the hard questions is an immense help in keeping my creative mind on track to get to the true heart of the story.

My dear friend Marcella Taylor does not just read books, she inhales them. Because of this, she has some keen insight into what will hold a reader's attention. In my case, it also helps that we have been friends for over twenty-five years. She can almost "think like Rosa," which is a scary thought for her. It is a comforting one for me though, as she often realizes where my thought process has gotten ahead of my typing speed.

Trained journalistically to limit punctuation, commas are a weakness of mine. Donna Stroupe is my compassionate reader who carefully checks "all things grammar" and keeps my commas on their toes. Her love of a story is evident in the thoughtful comments she makes during her review.

After having been sidekicks for the creation of the Legends of Graham Mansion series, Mary Lin Brewer has probably read my writing more times than anyone. I am very appreciative that she has taken the time to cast her eyes on this journey and give me some "delicious" feedback to consider.

The final person who reads my stories before I undertake the last edits is Carole Bybee. Despite the many reads that the story has undergone by then, Carole's keen skills find a few more errors or raise much needed questions of clarity. She also looks at the "big picture" of the story and helps to surmise if there are missing links which might confuse a reader.

Some say, you should not judge a book by its cover. I disagree! The wonderfully colorful and captivating covers for this series were designed by Cassy Roop of Pink Ink Designs (www.pinkindesigns.com). Even though Cassy and I have never met in person, she quickly understood what my vision was for this series and made the covers come to life. Her talented fingers are also behind the formatting of these books.

Every girl should be like Tremble and have her own Protector. Mine agreed to do that over twenty years ago. His patience during the writing process is very much appreciated as there are probably more "sandwich nights" than he would like.

Many thanks to all those wonderful readers who will take this journey with Tremble. I appreciate your feedback and loyalty. You are the reason I write.

ABOUT THE AUTHOR

Rosa Lee Jude began creating her own imaginary worlds at an early age. While her career path has included stints in journalism, marketing, hospitality & tourism and local government, she is most at home at a keyboard spinning yarns of fiction and creative non-fiction. She lives in the beautiful mountains of Southwest Virginia with her patient husband and very spoiled rescue dog.

The Enchanted Journey is Rosa Lee's second series. She is also the co-author of the award-winning time-travel series, the Legends of Graham Mansion. Learn more about her writing life at RosaLeeJude.com.

www.ingramcontent.com/pod-product-compliance
Lightning Source LLC
Chambersburg PA
CBHW020634260626
47157CB00008B/2730